W9-BXV-439

**"Uh, why don't you wait here?"
Isaac stopped in the hall,
clearly not wanting Leah to tag along.
"We'll be back in a few minutes."**

What was with the sudden secrecy? She suppressed a sting of hurt. She didn't like the way Isaac was trying to put her off, and had no intention of sitting around and waiting for him. She squared her shoulders and tucked a stray curl behind her ear. "No way. I'm coming with you."

Isaac stared at her for a long moment, a flash of helplessness, or maybe it was frustration, darkening his features before he threw his hands in the air. "Fine, suit yourself."

"I will." She trailed behind the two men, her stomach twisting with every step. Then she saw it—a small hole in the center of the windshield. And she knew without being told that it had been made by a bullet.

Someone had taken a shot at Isaac.

Books by Laura Scott

Love Inspired Suspense

The Thanksgiving Target
Secret Agent Father
The Christmas Rescue
Lawman-in-Charge
Proof of Life
Identity Crisis
Twin Peril
Undercover Cowboy
Her Mistletoe Protector
*Wrongly Accused
*Down to the Wire
*Under the Lawman's Protection

*SWAT: Top Cops

LAURA SCOTT

grew up reading faith-based romance books by Grace Livingston Hill, but as much as she loved the stories, she longed for a bit more mystery and suspense. She is honored to write for the Love Inspired Suspense line, where a reader can find a heartwarming journey of faith amid the thrilling danger.

Laura lives with her husband of twenty-five years and has two children, a daughter and a son, who are both in college. She works as a critical-care nurse during the day at a large level-one trauma center in Milwaukee, Wisconsin, and spends her spare time writing romance.

Please visit Laura at laurascottbooks.com, as she loves to hear from her readers.

UNDER THE LAWMAN'S PROTECTION

LAURA SCOTT

HARLEQUIN® LOVE INSPIRED® SUSPENSE

Recycling programs
for this product may
not exist in your area.

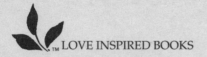 LOVE INSPIRED BOOKS

ISBN-13: 978-0-373-67654-5

Under the Lawman's Protection

Copyright © 2015 by Laura Iding

www.Harlequin.com

Printed in U.S.A.

He will cover you with his feathers,
and under his wings you will find refuge;
His faithfulness will be your shield and rampart.
—*Psalms* 91:4

This book is dedicated to my friend Olga Lita.
Thanks, Olga, for the wonderful support
you've provided over the years. Your friendship
means more to me than you'll ever know.

ONE

Swat team member Isaac Morrison paused outside the sheriff's-department headquarters and replayed the garbled voice-mail message for the third time.

Ice...cover blown...danger...help Leah and Ben...

The voice sounded like his buddy Shane "Hawk" Hawkins, and the use of his old nickname, Ice, gave credence to the fact that Hawk had left the message despite the unknown phone number. Was Hawk calling from a throwaway phone? Possibly. Isaac had tried to return the call twice, but it wouldn't go through.

Strange to be hearing from Hawk now, when they hadn't really been in touch for the past sixteen months, but the urgency in Hawk's static-filled message was impossible to ignore.

What in the world was going on? Isaac jogged to his Jeep, located in the far corner of the parking lot beneath a street lamp, his brain whirling with possibilities. Leah was Hawk's sister, and if he remembered correctly, Ben was her young son. By now the boy would be about five or so, and the thought that they might be in danger spurred Isaac into action. He revved up his Jeep and headed toward the interstate, wincing a bit at the fact that the time was approaching eight o'clock at night.

Hawk had left the message well over an hour ago. Isaac had had his phone on silent during his most recent tactical situation. He'd been called in as a negotiator at a local bank, where a drug addict had held a woman hostage in order to get money to fund his habit. Thankfully, they'd managed to take down the man before he shot or injured any innocent bystanders.

A good day for the Milwaukee County SWAT team, but the brief moment of satisfaction quickly evaporated with this latest threat. What if Isaac was already too late to protect Leah and Ben? He stomped on the accelerator, pushing the speed limit. He knew that Hawk's sister was the only family his buddy had left in the world, and the two were extremely close. The situation had to be serious for Hawk to call for help.

Isaac had met Hawk twelve years ago at Saint Jermaine's Youth Center, which was basically a school for delinquent teens, and during their first month there Hawk had saved his life. They'd been friends ever since, but Hawk had never asked for anything from him.

Until now.

Isaac hoped that Leah was still living in the same small home he remembered, located just inside the city limits. If she'd moved since the last time he saw her, he was in trouble, because he couldn't even remember her married name. Nelson? Nichols? Even though her husband had died roughly four years ago, he was pretty sure she hadn't remarried. Otherwise why would Hawk call him? Surely he would have contacted her new husband if she had one.

Isaac drove through the dark, damp March night, wondering if Leah would even remember him. He'd met her only a few times, and the last occasion must have been at her husband's funeral. The only good thing now was that he was still wearing his uniform, so at least she would be able to recognize him as one of the good guys.

Ironic that he and Hawk had both turned their troubled lives around to go into law enforcement. Hawk had taken a job with the City of Milwaukee Police Department, while Isaac had gone the route of joining the Milwaukee County Sheriff's Department. As they were located in two completely different jurisdictions, their paths hadn't crossed in the line of duty.

Hawk had mentioned that his cover was blown,

so he must have been investigating something serious while being undercover. But what? It would have helped to have some idea of the source of potential danger.

As he approached Leah and Ben's house, located at the bottom of a dead-end street, Isaac cut his headlights and slowed to a stop several yards away from the end of her driveway.

For a long moment he sat there, watching for any signs of life. But the windows were dark, and from the street he couldn't see any hint of light or movement inside. At eight-thirty on a Friday night, it was hard to believe Leah and Ben would be already asleep.

Either they weren't home yet or he was too late to save them.

Every nerve in his body rebelled at that thought, so he decided to investigate. He reached up to pull the bulb out of the dome light and then slipped out of his Jeep, hugging the shadows as he made his way closer to Leah's small house. In contrast, her yard was spacious and boasted several tall trees, one with a tire swing hanging from a thick branch. Seeing the swing reminded him of his dead son, and for a moment the pain of losing Jeremy nearly sent Isaac to his knees. He missed his son so much, but forced himself to concentrate on the task at hand. He tore his gaze from the swing, sweeping a wide glance across the yard to make sure that nothing was out of place.

No signs of a crime didn't mean one hadn't taken place. The warning itch along the back of his neck couldn't be ignored.

Moving slowly, he made his way around to the back of the house. There were still no lights anywhere and all was quiet. Leah didn't have anyone living to her left, but the neighbors to the right must be home, based on the blue glow of a television set in what appeared to be a living room. Surely if something had happened here, they would have been alerted.

He checked the back door to verify it was locked. He made a mental note to tell Leah she needed motion-sensor lights mounted in the backyard as well as out front above the garage. He was a little surprised that Hawk hadn't already taken care of that. Isaac rounded the corner of the house and abruptly stopped in his tracks, flattening himself against the siding when he saw a figure dressed from head to toe in black. The man had a ski mask covering his face, and he was stealthily making his way through Leah's front yard.

Hawk was right. Leah and Ben were in danger!

Isaac wished he'd asked a few of his SWAT teammates to come along, especially Caleb or Deck, but it was too late for that. Even if he called them, they were forty-five minutes away, and there wasn't a second to waste. He pulled his weapon and crouched low, trying to keep the intruder in his line of vision.

He considered calling 911 for backup, but feared the masked man would hear him. Using a cell phone, he'd have to give the dispatcher his location and even soft, muffled sounds carried loudly through the night. Right now, Isaac had the element of surprise on his side.

But he froze when the intruder hid alongside the large oak tree, the one with the tire swing hanging from it.

Clearly, the masked man was waiting for Leah and Ben.

Belatedly, Isaac noticed a pair of headlights approaching along the street, growing brighter and brighter as the car neared the house. The vehicle was an older-model sedan, but with the lights in his eyes, he couldn't tell for sure if the driver was male or female.

The possibility that Leah and Ben were coming home at this exact moment sent a shiver down his back. Had the masked man been following them? Or had his timing been pure luck?

Isaac didn't believe in coincidences. And he couldn't help wondering if the guy in black had a partner waiting somewhere nearby. He hadn't seen anyone, but that didn't mean someone wasn't still out there.

Isaac stayed at the corner of the house, his eyes trained on the oak tree. He had to assume the masked man would wait until the most opportune time to attack. The sedan pulled into the driveway and idled outside the garage. Isaac thought it was odd that the garage door didn't open, especially after several seconds passed.

Then he saw the driver's door open.

The events unraveled in slow motion. The masked intruder made his move, darting out from behind the tree and roughly grabbing the arm of the woman who'd gotten out of the car.

No! Isaac sprinted across the yard toward them. "Stop! Police!"

In a heartbeat, the man in black spun around, holding Leah in front of him as a hostage. Isaac froze when he saw he was pointing a gun at her temple. Her eyes were wide with terror and she kept glancing helplessly at the car, where her son was crying. Isaac couldn't afford to give him any reason to shoot.

"Look, no one has to get hurt here, okay?" He used his best negotiating tone and lifted his hands, pointing his weapon upward, indicating he wasn't going to shoot, either. If the masked man did have a partner, Isaac was dead meat, but there wasn't much he could do about it now.

Maybe the people watching television next door would hear the commotion and call the cops? He could only hope.

Isaac forced himself to calm down enough to go through the techniques he'd perfected over the years. "Listen, I'm sure this is just a big misunderstanding. Why don't you let the woman go?"

The masked man glanced around frantically, either looking for help or trying to figure out where Isaac had come from and if he had backup. The second thought gave him hope that the intruder didn't have a partner hidden out in the darkness. "Get out of here," the man said in a rough, muffled tone. "This isn't your business."

"I'm sorry, but I can't do that." Isaac tried to hold the man's gaze, but it wasn't easy in the darkness. The dome light of the sedan was the only illumination aside from the quarter moon hanging low in the sky. "I'm a cop and I can't let you hurt this woman. Why don't you tell me what you want? I'm sure we can work something out."

"Go away or I'll shoot."

Isaac knew the key to negotiating was to find some sort of common ground. Not easy to do when you knew nothing about the stranger holding a gun. But he sensed the guy didn't want to shoot Leah or would have done so already. That might be something to work with. "Please put the gun down. I have backup coming in less than five minutes. If you put the gun down, I promise no one will get hurt."

The masked man ignored him, glancing around as if trying to figure out his next move.

Isaac eased forward, still holding his hands up. Leah's pale face surrounded by a cloud of dark curls looked scared to death, and he blocked the image from his mind. If he allowed himself to worry about her, he'd mess this up. He had to remain focused on the intruder.

Unfortunately, Isaac had absolutely no clue what was going on, which had him at a distinct disadvantage. "Do you want money? Is that it? I'll give you my wallet if you'll let the woman go."

"Stop talking!" The masked man was losing control of the situation, and Isaac knew he had to find a way to make that crack in the guy's plan work to his advantage.

Inside the car, Ben was crying out for his mommy, and the noise seemed to be grating on the gunman's nerves. Isaac risked a glance inside the vehicle, and suddenly the man made his move.

"Take her!" he shouted. With a herculean push, he threw Leah away from him and turned to run.

Isaac had little choice but to grab Leah, preventing her from hitting the ground. She clutched him tightly as he stared over her shoulder as the man in black disappeared in the darkness.

As much as he wanted to chase after him, Isaac

stayed right where he was. He held Leah steady, knowing his priority needed to be protecting Hawk's sister and her son.

Leah Nichols closed her eyes for a moment, silently thanking God for keeping her safe. But she couldn't understand why the masked man had tried to kidnap her in the first place. What was going on? She had no idea, but couldn't shake the idea that whoever the guy with the gun was, he'd be back.

She had to get Ben out of here now! She needed to get someplace safe and to call her brother. Shane would protect her and her son.

Leah shoved away from the cop, trying to pull herself together. "Thank you," she murmured before turning back to the car, where Ben was still crying in the backseat. "Hey, Ben, I'm here. It's okay. We're fine."

"Leah, you and Ben should come with me."

She spun toward the cop, shaken by the fact that he knew their names. "Who are you?" she demanded. "And why are you here, anyway?"

"Don't you remember me? Isaac Morrison? I'm friends with your brother, Hawk, er, Shane. He sent me here to look after you."

Leah narrowed her gaze and shook her head. She vaguely remembered Hawk's friend Ice, also known as Isaac, but hadn't seen him in years.

Since her husband's funeral? Maybe. Yet could she really be sure this cop was who he said he was? She had only a vague memory of Shane's friend, but his height and his military-short, sandy-brown hair did seem familiar.

On the other hand, it seemed strange to her that Shane wouldn't come to help her himself. Or send one of his buddies, such as his partner from the force. This cop's uniform wasn't at all similar to the type that her brother used to wear. A fact that put her on edge.

"I appreciate your help, really, but I'll be fine on my own. Thanks anyway."

She slid back into her vehicle, intending to leave, but the cop grabbed her door before she could get it shut. "Leah, I don't know what's going on, but it's pretty clear you need protection. I swear I'm not going to hurt you or your son."

Leah battled a wave of helplessness. Should she really trust this guy?

"Here, listen to this message." The cop hunkered down next to her, playing with his phone. Abruptly, a brief static-filled message blared from the speaker.

Ice...cover blown...danger...help Leah and Ben...

The words sent a chill down her spine. She recognized Shane's voice, and the fact that her brother was clearly in trouble concerned her. "You need to help Shane," she blurted out. "I'll go to a hotel or something, but you need to help my brother."

But the cop was shaking his head. "No, I'm not leaving you and Ben alone. Don't you understand how much danger you're in? How long do you think it will take the bad guy to track your car? He was waiting here for you when you got home, and I'm sure he knows what type of vehicle you're driving. He probably even has the license-plate number."

Shiver after shiver racked her body and she knew with certainty the cop was right. Leah had taken Ben to a birthday party for one of his classmates at the Fun Zone. How had the masked man known what time to expect her? And why hadn't her garage door opened?

Belatedly, she realized that the light she'd left burning over the kitchen sink was also out. Had the gunman cut the power? She couldn't think of any other explanation.

"Leah, please." The cop reached out to gently cover her hand with his, and she forced herself to meet his intense gaze. "Do you want to see my ID to prove I'm Isaac Morrison? I know it's been a long time, but you have to believe I'm not going to hurt you."

She knew he was right and tried to calm her frayed nerves. "I'm sorry to be so paranoid," she murmured apologetically. "I'm just a bit rattled after everything that's happened."

Isaac smiled, and the expression softened his features, making her realize how handsome he was. Had he always been? Or had she just not noticed until now?

"You're entitled to be rattled," he assured her. "Let's get you and Ben someplace safe for tonight and then I'll see if I can get in touch with your brother. We'll discuss our next steps in the morning."

Tears pricked her eyes at his obvious concern. He'd saved her life tonight, and instead of saying thank you, she'd snapped at him. Of course they needed to leave, and right away. If the gunman knew what she was driving, she and Ben weren't safe.

She sniffed, blinked back her tears and nodded. "Sounds good. Thank you, Isaac. For everything."

"No problem." He rose to his feet. "Why don't you grab Ben and I'll take care of his booster seat?"

She slid out of the car and tucked her keys in her jacket pocket before heading around to the opposite side to get Ben. The cop followed and waited patiently until she had lifted her son in her arms before reaching for the car seat.

"Is that your Jeep parked on the road?" she asked.

"Yes. Wait for me, though." He tucked the

booster seat under his arm and then lightly grasped her arm, escorting her down the street, sweeping his gaze over the area as if ready for anything.

The idea that the gunman might not have been alone made her stomach twist with fear. Although if he'd had help, wouldn't that person have come forward to even the odds?

Maybe, maybe not. Killing a cop was something most criminals tried to avoid, at least according to what Shane was always telling her. But then again, her brother often downplayed just how dangerous his job was, especially since he worked in a district that handled the highest rate of violent crime. Shane knew that she'd purposefully chosen a man who wasn't a cop for a husband because of the fact that their father had been killed in the line of duty. Not that marrying a lawyer had helped her any. Elliot had been killed by a drunk driver, despite his *safe* job.

She pushed aside a wave of despair over losing her husband, knowing this wasn't the time to think about the past. She needed to concentrate on keeping her son safe.

Where was Shane now? She couldn't bear the thought of something happening to her brother. He had to be all right, he just had to be. Her son had already lost a father he didn't even remember. Surely God wouldn't take his uncle, too?

She stumbled and would have fallen if not for Isaac's hand beneath her arm.

"Leah?"

His low, gentle voice helped keep the panic at bay. She took a deep breath and let it out slowly. It had been a long time since she'd leaned on a man for support, and she couldn't deny appreciating the fact she wasn't alone. "I'm fine."

Isaac opened the Jeep door and quickly threaded the belt through Ben's booster seat. He stepped back, giving her room to get her son settled inside.

"I love you, Ben," she whispered, pressing a kiss to the top of his head.

"I love you, too, Mommy."

Tears threatened again, and since she wasn't the crying type, she had to assume that they were a delayed reaction from the horrific experience of being held at gunpoint. Her son was only five years old, but she was afraid he might have nightmares from seeing the gunman grab her. She brushed the dampness away as she climbed past her son so that she could sit in the back, next to him.

If Isaac was annoyed with her choice to stay in the rear rather than next to him, he didn't let on. He shut the door behind her and then jogged around to get into the driver's seat. He started the engine and glanced back at her. "Buckle up."

She reached for the seat belt a bit embarrassed that she hadn't remembered. As an E.R. nurse, she'd seen more than enough car-crash victims and normally the gesture was automatic. But nothing about this night was normal.

She rested her head back against the seat and closed her eyes. Almost instantly the memory of the masked man grabbing her from behind the wheel flashed in her brain, so she pried her eyelids open and stared out the window, willing the image away.

When Isaac slowed down to turn onto one of the main highways leading away from town, she frowned and leaned forward. "Where exactly are you taking us?" she asked.

"There's a hotel that isn't too far from our SWAT headquarters," he said, meeting her gaze in the rearview mirror.

"Why do we have to go all the way across town?" she asked. "There are plenty of hotels closer to my house."

"Yes, but I don't think staying close to your house is a wise thing to do right now." He was using the same calm, reasonable tone that he'd used with the gunman, and for some reason that irked her. "The guy knew where you lived and what time you were coming home. Trust me, the farther away we can get from your place, the better."

"I know, but what if Shane comes looking for me?" She couldn't understand why they had to go so far away.

"We'll let your brother know where we are," Isaac assured her. "Did that guy say anything to you before I arrived?"

She didn't really want to relive those moments, but understood that Isaac was only trying to get information. And she'd do whatever necessary to help her brother. She licked her dry lips. "He told me that if I screamed he'd shoot."

"I'm sorry you had to go through that."

The sincere note in her rescuer's voice made her eyes fill with tears, which she rapidly blinked away. She had to be strong, for Shane's sake as well as Ben's. She tried to recall every detail of her brief encounter. "The garage door wouldn't open and the light I left on above the kitchen sink was out, too. Do you think he cut the electricity?"

"Very possibly, but unfortunately, I didn't see him do anything like that. I only saw him hiding behind your big oak tree. Is it possible you were followed? I can't help wondering if he might have cut the power earlier."

The thought that she might have been followed to the birthday party at Fun Zone only put her more on edge. How could she not have noticed? Although why would she even look for someone following her? Being an E.R. nurse was hardly dangerous. And suddenly Leah was overwhelmed by a wave of helplessness. She closed her eyes again and prayed.

Please, Lord, thank You for saving me and Ben from the gunman. I ask that You keep Shane, Isaac, me and Ben safe in Your care. Amen.

Her emotions calmed down after her prayer, and for the first time since pulling into her driveway, she felt as if she was on the right path.

If her brother had sent Isaac to keep her and Ben safe, then Leah needed to trust his judgment. And to trust in God. She couldn't do this on her own.

"The place I'm taking you and Ben is called the Forty Winks Hotel." He captured her gaze in the rearview mirror. "It's a cute establishment. We've used it before. You and Ben will be safe there."

Safe. She liked the sound of that. Oddly enough, she was glad Isaac was here, protecting her and Ben.

But abruptly, the Jeep jerked sharply to the right, causing her to cry out in alarm. Isaac wrestled with the steering wheel in a vain attempt to stay on the road, but it was no use.

What was going on? Leah swallowed a scream and grabbed her son's hand, praying for God to watch over them and ignoring the way her seat belt bit sharply into her shoulder as the vehicle plunged into a ditch.

TWO

"Leah? Ben?" Isaac fought to get free of his seat belt so he could make sure his passengers were safe. "Are you both all right?"

Ben was crying and Leah was trying to console him. "Shh, Ben, we're okay. Everything's fine. Don't cry, sweetie. Please don't cry."

Hearing Ben sob ripped at his heart. Yet there wasn't time to waste. "We need to get out of here."

"What? Why?"

He didn't want to scare Leah more than she already was, but he believed someone had taken a shot at them. "Try to keep your head down and don't get out of the car yet, okay? I don't think this was an accident." He quickly called the dispatch center, giving the code for officer needing assistance. "We're not far from Highway 22," he informed them.

"Ten-four."

He hung up and then called Caleb's number. Thankfully, his teammate answered on the second ring. "You interrupted our family time," Caleb mumbled. "This better be important."

"I'm sorry, but I need backup," Isaac said. "I'm fairly certain someone caused me to crash my Jeep."

"All right, I'll grab Deck, too." Caleb didn't hesitate to come to his aid, and Isaac knew he was lucky to have friends like them. "Where are you?"

Isaac gave his location and then disconnected from the call, feeling better knowing the two men he trusted the most would be there soon. Of course, the dispatcher would send someone out as well, but Isaac needed members of the SWAT team to help him figure out exactly what they were dealing with.

"So you think someone made us crash?" Leah asked fearfully.

He glanced back at her, trying to figure out how much to say in front of Ben. "It's just a hunch, but yeah. The tires on this Jeep are brand-new and I didn't see anything on the road that could have caused this. Just stay down. I'm going to go out and make sure there isn't someone out there."

"Wait!" she cried as he was about to open his car door. "Don't go. Stay here with us."

He was torn between two impossible choices. If someone had shot out the tires on purpose, he couldn't just wait for that person to come and finish them off. Nor did he want to leave Leah and Ben here alone.

So far he wasn't doing the greatest job of keeping Hawk's sister and her son safe. If he'd been wearing his bulletproof gear he would be in better shape to go out to investigate.

Isaac peered out the window, trying to see if anyone was out there. Sitting here was making him crazy, so he decided doing something was better than nothing.

"I'm armed, Leah, so don't worry about me. I promise I'll do whatever it takes to keep you and Ben safe."

He could tell she wanted to protest, but she bit her lip and nodded. She pulled her son out of his booster seat and tucked him next to her, so that he was protected on either side. Then she curled her body around him. The fact that she would risk herself to protect Ben gave Isaac a funny feeling in the center of his chest.

Leah's actions were humbling. He hadn't been attracted to a woman in a long time, not since his wife had left him for a guy who turned out to be mentally unstable. A man who'd shot Becky, Jeremy and then himself in a fit of depressed anger.

But this wasn't the time to ruminate over the past. Isaac's ex-wife and son were gone and nothing in the world would bring them back. So Isaac would do the next best thing—protect Leah and Ben with his life if necessary.

Isaac hadn't replaced the bulb in the dome light, so he wasn't too worried about broadcasting his movements. He pushed open the driver's-side door and used it as a shield as he swept his gaze around, searching for any sign of danger. The country road he'd taken was deserted, which wasn't at all reassuring. He had to assume that someone had hidden in the trees along the opposite side of the road, waiting for his Jeep to show up so they could take a shot at him. The last thing he wanted to do was sit here and wait for yet another gunman to show up.

He was positive he hadn't been followed, which left only one option. The masked man must have known he was a sheriff's deputy, maybe by recognizing the uniform, and he'd come this way hoping to ambush him, since this was the main road leading to the sheriff's-department headquarters.

How much time did they have before there was another attempt to take Leah and Ben? Probably not much.

Isaac had to decide right now if they'd be safer outside or waiting in the Jeep. Normally he didn't have trouble making decisions.

But for some reason, he couldn't seem to get the image of the gunman holding Leah hostage out of his mind. The personal responsibility gnawed at him.

Outside the Jeep, he abruptly decided. For sure, they needed to get outside to hide, so they weren't sitting ducks.

He climbed back in and closed the door. "We're going to get out on the passenger side, okay? I'll go first and then you and Ben will follow."

Leah lifted her tearstained face and nodded. Her silent tears made him feel bad for her, but he forced himself to concentrate. Awkwardly, he climbed over the gearshift and then pushed open the passenger door. Staying behind the protection of the car, he opened the door to the back, taking the booster seat out first, to give Leah and Ben room to maneuver.

"Come on out," he said in a low voice.

Leah lifted Ben and handed him over. Isaac moved to the side, keeping the boy in front of him so that Ben was sandwiched between him and the car. Leah climbed out, too, and immediately reached for her son.

"Stay down," Isaac said, moving so that he was directly behind her.

"Where are we going?" she asked in a whisper.

Good question. There weren't streetlights, but the scant amount of lingering snow on the ground reflected the moonlight, making it brighter than he was comfortable with. "See that small cluster of trees?" He indicated an area directly behind him. "We're going to hide there."

Fear shimmered in her eyes, but she gave a jerky nod of agreement.

"You and Ben first. I'll protect you from behind. Ready? Let's go."

Leah clutched her son close and ran up the slippery embankment toward the trees, moving faster than he'd anticipated. Then again, adrenaline had a way of giving the body a boost when needed the most. He held his weapon ready and kept pace behind her.

When Leah and Ben were safe in the grove, Isaac gave a little sigh of relief. He was about to join them when his foot slipped on a patch of melting snow. He fell to his knees and felt something whiz past his head.

A bullet?

"Get down," he ordered hoarsely, practically throwing himself on top of Leah.

"What happened?" she asked in a muffled tone.

He didn't want to scare her, but he couldn't lie to her, either. "I'm pretty sure someone is shooting at us. Sit down at the base of this big tree and hold Ben in your lap. My backup will be here soon."

Leah did as he asked, sliding to the ground and hugging her boy close. Isaac could hear her murmuring something, and he leaned down, trying to hear what she was saying.

It was then he realized she was praying.

Dear Lord, keep us safe in Your care! Give Isaac the strength and the courage to defeat our enemy. We ask this in Christ the Lord. Amen.

Normally he wasn't the praying type, but right now, Isaac couldn't deny they needed all the help they could get. And if that meant praying, he was all for it.

Leah cuddled Ben close, whispering prayers as a way to keep them both calm. She felt terrible about how he had been crying on and off, clearly not understanding what was going on. To be fair, she didn't really understand, either.

Why would someone come after her and Ben? Not just once tonight, but twice? She was very grateful she was here with Isaac rather than being alone.

"There, do you hear that?" her brother's friend asked softly.

She couldn't hear anything beyond the thundering of her heart. She was about to shake her head when she heard the faint wail of a siren.

Help is on the way!

"Maybe you should call them and let them know where we are," she suggested.

"No, the light from my phone would be a beacon showing our location to the shooter. As it is, he already knows we're on the move. But from the angle of the bullet, he must still be up in the trees somewhere, which is good for us, as that means he isn't in the process of making his way over here on foot. Unless he has a partner."

"But why is he shooting at all? I don't understand."

Isaac scowled. "He was probably trying to take me out of the picture so that he had a clear path to get to you."

She swallowed hard, wishing she hadn't asked.

The radio on Isaac's lapel crackled and he quickly muffled the sound with his gloved hands. "ETA?" he whispered.

"Less than five."

"Shooter in the tree line on the south side of the street," he murmured. "Stay down."

"Ten-four."

Leah began reciting the Lord's Prayer. She could feel Isaac's gaze on her and she couldn't help wondering if he wasn't a Christian. Not that she should be surprised, because her brother went to church only when she forced the issue. And even then he mostly attended for Ben's sake.

"We're not beat yet," Isaac said when she'd finished her prayer. "We're going to be fine as soon as my teammates Caleb and Deck get here."

"I know. But praying keeps me calm. I take it you don't have the same experience?"

He gave a brief shake of his head and averted his gaze. "Nope. The only times I go to church are for weddings or funerals. And truth be told, in my line of work it's more of the latter."

She knew very well what he meant. Hadn't she learned that firsthand? Her father had died in the line of duty, as had one of his colleagues. And on top of that, she'd lost her husband to a drunk driver on his third DUI offense.

Too much loss for one person to handle.

Since the last thing she wanted to think about was the dangers associated with Shane's and Isaac's respective jobs, she twisted around so she could see the road.

"Red lights in the distance," Isaac murmured in his low, reassuring tone. "My team will be here soon."

"Thank You, Lord," she murmured.

"Amen," Ben said in a small voice. Her eyes welled up with tears at her son's sentiment. At that moment she was grateful she'd taken him to church every week.

"See, Ben? We're safe now."

"But, Mommy, I'm cold," he whined.

"I know, sweetie." She brushed her lips over Ben's forehead. "Mr. Isaac's friends will be here soon and then we'll be able to get into a warm car, okay?"

"We're hiding in a cluster of trees at your three o'clock," Isaac murmured into the radio.

"Ten-four."

"They're not going to search the trees across the street, are they?" Leah asked, trying not to be too blunt, for Ben's sake.

"No, getting you two to safety is our main priority."

Once again she was glad she wasn't out here alone. So far, Isaac had proved to be dedicated in his mission to protect her and Ben.

Maybe her brother had chosen wisely after all. Even though she never wanted to be married to a cop, especially seeing what her mother had gone through after losing her father, being helped by one who was determined to protect you wasn't all bad.

The red lights grew brighter and soon she saw two sheriff's-department vehicles park behind Isaac's ditched Jeep. First one dark figure climbed out of the car, dressed in full SWAT gear, and then a second figure joined him. Within minutes, they made their way over to their hiding spot amid the trees.

"Hey, Isaac, what's the deal? Haven't you had enough adventure for one day?" the shorter of the two asked in a low voice.

"Knock it off," he growled, not looking the least bit amused. "Listen, I need you and Caleb to create a wall of armor so that we can get Leah and Ben down to your vehicle. I'm fairly certain the shooter was on the other side of the road."

"No problem. We're ready."

"Okay, Leah, I want you to slowly stand up, while keeping your head down," Isaac instructed.

"Okay." Rising to her feet was easier said than done, since her legs had gone numb. Plus Isaac hadn't moved back very far, so there wasn't a lot of room to maneuver.

But then Caleb, or was it Declan, reached down and helped her up. Isaac stayed behind her, while the other officer took Ben. Clustered together as one, they slowly moved across the muddy terrain, heading in the direction of the vehicles. When they reached the nearest one, Leah set Ben on the rear seat and climbed in beside him. One of Isaac's friends brought over the booster seat and soon Ben was securely fastened inside.

"Stay here," Isaac said in a low voice. "The windows are bulletproof, so there's no reason to be afraid. We'll be out of here soon enough."

"Okay." She couldn't deny being relieved to know the windows were reinforced. But that didn't stop her from searching the trees across the street, looking for any sign of the masked man.

Isaac spoke to the other two officers outside for

a few minutes before he slid in behind the wheel.
He cranked the key and blasted the heat. "We'll
be leaving in a few minutes."

"W-what about y-your J-Jeep?" she asked, her
teeth chattering as her entire body began to shake.
Reaction from the night's events had finally hit
her, and she couldn't seem to get her body under
control.

"The guys will make sure it gets back to the
station. We want the crime-scene techs to take a
look at my rear tire. Not that there's much left to
examine."

Leah gave a jerky nod, unable to trust her voice
not to betray her. Isaac turned in his seat and
pinned her with a direct gaze.

"I'm going to make sure you and Ben get someplace safe for the rest of the night," he said in a
serious tone. "Okay?"

"S-sure." She could tell he was feeling bad
about everything that had just happened, but none
of this was his fault.

Of course, it wasn't exactly her fault, either.

She suppressed another shiver, wishing she
knew where her brother was. And couldn't help
wondering if she'd ever feel safe again.

Isaac inwardly winced when Leah wrapped her
arms around her abdomen as if trying to keep
herself from shaking.

He scrubbed his hands over his face, telling himself it was not a good idea to scoot in beside her to offer comfort. He'd managed to keep his distance from any romantic entanglements over the past few years, and this was hardly the time or the place to change his mind. Especially with his friend's sister, no matter how beautiful she was.

Still, he wished there was a way to ease Leah's fears. To let her know that she was handling this better than anyone could expect.

He shook his head at his foolishness and peered through the windshield. Having Caleb and Declan outside, trying to put the puzzle pieces together for him, didn't sit well. He wanted to be out there in the middle of the action.

But Hawk was his friend and Leah was his responsibility, not theirs, though they'd both offered to help in any way they could.

As soon as he had his charges in a safe place, Isaac would need to find a way to get in touch with Hawk. Someone wanted Leah and Ben, and the only thing that made sense to him was that they needed some leverage to draw his friend out of hiding.

Hawk had mentioned that his cover was blown, and Leah and Ben were in danger. But from whom? What in the world was Hawk involved in?

"Isaac?" Caleb rapped on the window. "You need to come out here and see this."

He lifted his hand to show he'd heard. He turned back toward Leah. "I'll only be a minute, okay?"

She nodded, but didn't meet his gaze. She looked so weary, as if she might keel over at any moment.

Guilt weighed heavily on his shoulders as he turned back and pushed open the driver's-side door. He followed Caleb over to his Jeep, where Deck was standing with a flashlight trained on the rear fender.

"What is it?" he asked.

"Check this out." Deck aimed his beam of light at the lower edge of the wheel well. "What do you think? Looks like a bullet hole to me."

Isaac stared in shock as the implication of the small round hole sank deep. "The shooter took two shots at the tire," he murmured slowly. "He must have missed the first time."

"Yeah, but not by much," Caleb pointed out. "And you both know how difficult it is to hit a tire on a moving vehicle. The average citizen could never pull this off. Our perp is a sharpshooter of some kind, maybe a sniper from the armed forces."

"Yeah," Isaac agreed grimly, turning to look up at his two closest friends. "Or maybe a cop, like us."

Caleb and Deck exchanged grim glances and

then nodded. "You could be right," Caleb acknowledged. "It wouldn't be the first time we encountered a dirty cop on the force."

No, it wouldn't. Isaac stared at the small round hole in the fender. Keeping Leah and Ben safe wouldn't be nearly as easy if they had a cop or some other guy with military training on his tail.

But failure was not an option.

THREE

Leah was relieved when Isaac returned to the sheriff's-deputy SUV after just a few short minutes. "C-can we leave now?" she asked.

"Yes," he responded shortly, as if he wasn't happy about something. He put the SUV in gear and pulled out onto the highway. The silence stretched between them as Isaac drove, taking a series of turns that made her wonder if he was making sure no one was following.

The warmth from the heater finally penetrated her chilled body and she relaxed against the seat, feeling safe at least for the moment.

She peeked over at her son. Ben's eyes had drifted closed, as he was no doubt exhausted after his crying jag. She was glad he was able to get some rest. "What did Caleb want to show you?" she asked in a low tone.

Isaac's eyes briefly met hers in the rearview mirror. "Evidence."

"Of what?"

There was another long silence. "A bullet hole located in the Jeep's fender."

She swallowed hard. Suspecting that the tire was shot on purpose and knowing beyond a shadow of a doubt were two different things. All because someone wanted to get to her and Ben? Why? What in the world had Shane gotten mixed up in? "We need to talk to my brother," she murmured.

"I know. I tried to call him earlier, but he didn't pick up, and there wasn't a voice-mail box set up on his phone, so I couldn't leave him a message. I'll try again later."

She was surprised to note it was only about ten-fifteen at night. For some reason, the hour felt much later. Or maybe it was just that so much had happened in such a short time. "Are we still going to the Forty Winks Hotel?"

Isaac shook his head. "No, I've decided to go to a different place Deck suggested. Both Caleb and he have used the Forty Winks before, and right now I'd rather go someplace with fewer ties to the SWAT team, just to be on the safe side. Deck has reserved two adjoining rooms for us."

Adjoining rooms? She hadn't thought much beyond getting to the hotel, but now realized she should have known that Isaac wouldn't just leave her and Ben there alone. Of course he'd want to stay close at hand, especially after this latest close call in the Jeep. Two attempts to shoot them in less than two hours must be some sort of record. She was glad she wasn't going to be totally alone. And having adjoining rooms would provide some modicum of privacy.

She watched the street signs, trying to familiarize herself with the area. Most of the Wisconsin-winter snow had melted, leaving a slushy, muddy mess in its wake. A quarter moon hung in the sky, but the stars were faint and difficult to see, no doubt because Isaac was driving them closer to the city.

Fifteen minutes later, he pulled into the parking lot of a place called the American Lodge. She thought the Forty Winks Hotel sounded better, but obviously she wasn't in a position to argue. The Lodge wasn't very big, but there were two stories. She leaned forward and tapped Isaac's shoulder. "I'd rather be on the ground floor if possible," she said. "Ben is at the age where he climbs everything, and I don't want to risk him going over the balcony."

"No problem," Isaac murmured. He drew up in front of the lobby. "Stay here and wait for me, okay?"

She nodded and rested against the seat cushion, wishing she had a change of clothes with her. Her jeans were splattered with mud from their mad dash to the trees. Hopefully, Isaac would ask for some basic toiletries at the front desk.

Ben was still asleep in his booster seat and she wished she didn't have to wake him up. After everything they'd been through, he deserved a little peace.

Isaac returned from the lobby with two key packets in his hand. He handed one to her and then drove around the side of the building. "We're in rooms 10 and 12, last two on the first floor."

"Okay." She turned, released the seat belt and eased Ben out of the booster seat.

"Do you want me to carry him inside?" Isaac offered.

She hesitated, but then nodded. The adrenaline rush had faded, leaving her feeling shaky and weak. Her muscles felt sore, as if she'd run some sort of marathon rather than a short sprint to a grove of trees. She climbed out her side of the vehicle while Isaac opened the other back door.

He gently lifted Ben out of his car seat and carried him toward their room. Leah pulled the plastic key card out and unlocked the door. After flipping on the light, she stood back so that Isaac could set Ben on one of the two double beds, choosing the one closest to the bathroom.

The room was clean, but smelled a bit musty,

as if it hadn't been used in a few days. Still, she was grateful to be here.

"The clerk at the desk provided a few toiletries for us." Isaac fished the items out of his coat pocket and set toothbrushes, toothpaste and a comb on the dresser. Then he crossed over to the connecting door. "I need you to leave this unlocked, okay? I'll open my side, as well."

She nodded wearily. "I understand. Thanks again, for everything."

Isaac stared at her for a long moment, his dark eyes intense. The strange awareness between them unnerved her and she took a step backward, as if more distance would help. He looked as if he wanted to say something more, but then he turned and strode toward the door. "If you need anything at all, let me know."

"I will."

When the door closed behind him, she felt a momentary flash of panic. Ridiculous, since he was only going right next door. She crossed over and opened the connecting door, listening for sounds from the other room. It didn't take long for Isaac to unlock and open his door.

"Are you okay?" he asked when he saw her standing there, obviously waiting.

She forced a smile, hoping he wouldn't notice her blush. "Yes, of course. Good night."

"Good night."

She left a one-inch gap in the door before making her way over to Ben. Carefully, so as to not wake him up, she removed his winter coat, hat and shoes. She left his long-sleeved T-shirt and jeans on in lieu of pajamas. Setting the outer clothing aside, she bent over and pressed a kiss to the top of his head, thanking God once again for keeping her son safe.

Ben wiggled around, muttering something incomprehensible before burrowing into the pillow. She pulled the covers up over him and then made her way to the bathroom. She washed her hands and face, then dabbed at the mud splatters on her jeans with a soapy washcloth. She used the toothbrush and toothpaste, but didn't bother with the comb, since her naturally curly hair would be better served with a brush. She went back into the room and sat on the edge of her bed, cradling her head in her hands.

She needed to get some sleep, but couldn't make herself crawl in between the sheets. Instead, her mind whirled with questions. Where was Shane? What had he stumbled into? Was he hiding? Hurt? Or worse?

After a brief internal debate, she stood up and went back over to the connecting doors, tapping lightly to get Isaac's attention.

"What's wrong?" He leaped to his feet, instantly on alert.

"Nothing," she quickly assured him. "I can't sleep."

Isaac nodded and sank back down on his seat. "I know. I tried calling Hawk again, but there's no answer."

"That doesn't sound good," she said with a frown.

"He knows how to reach me," Isaac pointed out. "I'm sure he'll get in touch soon."

She stared at him for a long moment, trying to gauge his mood. "I feel like we need to do something to help him. Something more than sitting here."

Isaac gestured to the chair across from him and then rubbed his hand across the shadow of his beard. "Do you have any idea what your brother is investigating?"

She sank into the chair, trying to remember anything Shane had said. "Not really. He doesn't talk about his job very much. I know he was assigned a new partner about four months ago, some guy by the name of Trey."

Isaac's eyes lit up. "Do you know his last name?"

She pressed her fingers against her temples, trying to remember. "Something like a tree," she murmured, thinking back to the conversation she'd had with Shane. "Birchwood. Trey Birchwood."

Isaac leaned forward. "What else did he say? Did he get along with Birchwood?"

"Shane mentioned Trey was from another district and that the guy was okay." She shrugged and grimaced. "You have to understand that Shane didn't ever say anything negative about his job. He kept all the dangerous details to himself."

"Understandable that he wouldn't want you to worry," Isaac said. "But surely he would have said something if he had real concerns about his new partner."

"Not necessarily," she argued. "Shane glosses over everything bad because he knows I really don't like the fact that he's in constant danger." Admitting her fears out loud wasn't easy, but if it helped her brother, the embarrassment was well worth it. "When he mentioned his new partner, his tone was rather offhand. I wish I knew if there was some sort of rift between them, but I don't because I never asked." She was angry with herself now, although she certainly hadn't known that she'd end up in danger.

Isaac held her gaze for a long minute and she tried not to squirm in her seat. "I take it you don't approve of your brother's career choice?"

She took a deep breath and let it out slowly.

"Did Shane happen to mention that our dad died in the line of duty?"

Isaac nodded. "Yes, he told me back when we were at Saint Jermaine's."

"Well, then you know that Shane went a little crazy after our dad died. That's when he started getting into trouble. I'm pretty sure he got caught up in drugs for a bit, although he never admitted that to me. I know he was arrested, and thankfully, the judge sentenced him to Saint Jermaine's rather than sending him to jail."

"Yeah, I was grateful for the chance to go there, as well."

She was a little surprised to know that Isaac and Shane had both been at Saint Jermaine's, but then realized she shouldn't be. Shane was three years older than her and she had been only fourteen when he was sent to the boys' school. And much of that time, the year or two after her father's death, was nothing more than a blur, especially once their mother started hitting the bottle. Her mom had died while Leah was in college, and from that point on, she and Shane had depended on each other.

Glancing at Isaac, she was glad to know he'd been given the same opportunity to turn his life around as her brother had. And it was interesting that they both had chosen law enforcement.

She gave herself a mental shake. Why was she

concerned about Isaac's life? She'd married Elliot right out of nursing school and lost him barely two years later. She had no intention of opening herself up to that kind of hurt again.

"Well, thanks, Leah," Isaac said, breaking into her thoughts. "I'll see what I can find out about your brother's new partner. Now, do me a favor and try to get some sleep."

He was right—there was nothing else she could do tonight. And he obviously wanted her to leave, so she rose to her feet and walked toward the connecting door. She glanced back at Isaac over her shoulder and was disconcerted to find him watching her intently. "Good night," she murmured before slipping through the opening to her own room.

As she crawled into bed, she told herself that she'd imagined the disappointment reflected on Isaac's face when she'd mentioned not liking her brother's career choice. And if she hadn't imagined it, she was still glad he understood exactly where she was coming from.

They might have been thrown together by circumstances outside their control, but she knew very well that as soon as they found her brother, they'd go their separate ways.

And truthfully, she couldn't help hoping that happened sooner than later. Because she wasn't ready to even consider getting romantically involved again.

Not now and maybe not ever.

Isaac watched Leah walk away, telling himself that it was a good thing there couldn't be anything more between them than friendship. So what if she was so beautiful it made his gut ache? It wasn't as if he intended to get married again, not after his first wife had left him, taking their son with her. And when his ex-wife's new boyfriend went crazy, killing her and then Jeremy and then himself, the hole in Isaac's heart had gotten wider and deeper.

Two years had passed but he still missed his son every single day. And deep down, he hadn't found a way to forgive himself for his wife's leaving him. He should have known she wasn't happy. She'd always told him he worked too many hours, but he hadn't listened.

And now it was too late to right the wrong.

Maybe his teammates Caleb and Declan had managed to find a way to make their relationships work, even with their crazy schedules, but Isaac had failed and wasn't interested in trying again.

So why was he disappointed to find out Leah wasn't interested in someone like him?

He shook off the bizarre feeling and made a call to the Fifth District asking for Trey Birchwood.

He was told the cop was off duty for the weekend, so that wasn't much help. It was Friday night, so it could be that Trey was actually off work. Or it could be that he'd specifically requested time off for some unknown reason.

Talking to Trey might not offer any insight as to what Hawk was involved with, but Isaac needed to try. That was the only lead he had at the moment.

He prowled the room, glancing out the window to scan the parking lot, making sure no one was lurking around. The lot was mostly empty and he'd parked the SUV in front of his door, rather than closer to Leah's. And he'd backed it in, so they could drive off in a hurry if needed.

He reached for his phone to check in with Caleb and Deck, nearly dropping it when the cell vibrated in his hand. His pulse jumped as he recognized the number of Hawk's throwaway phone. "Hawk? Are you okay?"

"Are Leah and Ben safe?" His friend's voice was grave, and Isaac couldn't help but wonder if his buddy was injured.

"Yes, but there have already been two attempts to get them. A gunman showed up at their house and then someone else shot out the tire on my Jeep. What's going on?"

"My cover is blown." Static filled the line and

Isaac strained to listen. "Don't trust anyone in my district, understand?"

"Not even Trey Birchwood?"

More static, but then Hawk's voice came through. "No. Not until I know more about what's going on."

Isaac couldn't tell if Hawk normally got along well with his new partner or not, but since he wasn't trusting any of the guys from his district, it was a moot point. "You have to give me something to go on. I want to help you."

"You are helping me by keeping Leah and Ben safe. These guys will do anything to find me, including using my family as bait."

Isaac knew his initial instincts were correct. The gunman wanted Leah and Ben alive, to draw Hawk out of hiding.

"Remember Saint Jermaine's?" Hawk asked, breaking into his thoughts.

Isaac frowned. "Yeah. What about it?"

"There were a couple of guys who bragged about running illegal guns."

"I remember." The tiny hairs on the back of Isaac's neck lifted in alarm. "Are you investigating some sort of illegal gun trade?"

"Yes. I was approached by an agent with the ATF, and it's bigger than I anticipated. I'm convinced there are dirty cops involved."

So he was right about the sharpshooter being

an officer. Isaac knew there were rare occasions when cops turned bad, and investigating those situations was always tricky.

Still, knowing the Bureau of Alcohol, Tobacco and Firearms was involved made him feel a little better. At least Hawk wasn't hanging out there totally alone. "Talk to me. What can I do?"

"Keep my sister and her boy safe. I'll figure out the rest myself."

"What's the name of your ATF contact?" Isaac pressed.

There was a pause. "Cameron Walker, but don't contact him. Not yet. I'll let you know if I need anything more."

"Where are you?"

"Hiding. Don't even try to find me. I'm constantly on the move."

Isaac wished there was something he could do for his friend. "Look, I have a couple of guys on my team that I'd trust with my life," he said quickly. "We can help you. You can't do this alone, buddy."

"I have to go." Hawk abruptly disconnected the call, leaving Isaac battling a wave of helplessness.

He didn't know much more than he had before Hawk phoned, other than to have his suspicions confirmed about why the gunman had gone after Leah and Ben. Still, hearing that Hawk was investigating illegal weapons under the supervision of the ATF was something. Most criminals on the streets knew exactly where to find guns that they wanted, since they were practically everywhere. Isaac couldn't even begin to think of where to start, especially considering Hawk's claim that he'd stumbled upon something big.

Isaac stretched out on the bed fully dressed, thinking about the little bit Hawk had revealed. He remembered his team had been called to a mall shooting about a week ago. He'd been the negotiator for the tactical situation, while Caleb had functioned as the sharpshooter. The weapon they'd recovered at the scene had been obviously illegal, with the serial numbers filed off.

Isaac sat up, knowing the gun was likely still in the evidence room. The possible connection was thin, but still worth investigating.

He picked up his phone, but then hesitated. It was well after midnight and the gun wasn't going anywhere tonight. No sense in dragging Caleb or Deck out now.

It could wait until morning.

Isaac turned the television on low, scanning the various news channels. Unfortunately, no baseball spring-training games were on this late at night.

The sound of a car engine caught his attention. He rolled off the bed, grabbed his weapon and crossed over to the window. He peered through the slight opening in the curtains, trying to see what had caused the noise.

The parking lot appeared deserted, but then he saw the quick flash of taillights moving away.

Could be nothing, but after the troubling conversation with Hawk, Isaac didn't want to assume anything, especially if dirty cops were involved. He stared at the now-empty parking lot for a minute and then eased back, walking toward the connecting door, intending to get Leah and Ben up. They wouldn't like leaving again, but he'd rather play it safe than sorry.

He'd taken only two steps when the sound of breaking glass echoed through the night. He stumbled and glanced over his shoulder at the same time his eyes started to burn.

Tear gas!

He dived through the connecting door, slamming it shut behind him. He needed to get Leah and Ben out of here now!

FOUR

Leah woke up with a start when Isaac came barreling through the connecting door into their room. She gasped and stared in shock when he shut it behind him and then ripped the comforter off her bed and stuffed it along the bottom edge of the door.

"Grab Ben. We need to get out of here."

Leah didn't question Isaac's command as her eyes began to burn. She scrambled out of bed, grateful she'd slept in her clothes, and quickly roused her son. She tugged his winter clothes on despite his sleepy protest.

"Use these to cover your faces," Isaac said, handing her two wet towels. She threw one over her shoulder and drew Ben up against it, then draped another around her neck so that it was close to her mouth. It was the best she could do while carrying her son. "This way," Isaac said, urging her toward the bathroom.

It didn't take long for Isaac to break open the

small window there. "I'm going out first so that I can help the two of you through, okay?"

She clutched Ben close and nodded. It wasn't easy for Isaac to get his broad-shouldered frame through the small opening, and she let out a sigh of relief when he finally made it.

"Okay, Ben, it's your turn." Isaac said.

"No, don't wanna go!" he wailed, grabbing her around the neck and hanging on tight.

It nearly broke her heart to pull him away. "We have to, Ben. Mr. Isaac is out there to catch you, and I'll hold you once we're outside, okay?"

"No-o-o," he cried, deep wrenching sobs that tore at her.

Leah forced herself to push him through the window into Isaac's waiting arms. She wiped her own tears away before attempting to climb after her son. She could hear Isaac whispering soothing words to Ben, and he stopped crying except for the occasional hiccuping sniffle.

Isaac's strong hand guided her through the opening and soon she was on solid ground. She took Ben and tossed the wet towels aside, gulping in deep breaths of fresh air.

"See those trees fifty feet from here?" Isaac asked in a low whisper, his breath tickling her ear. She swallowed hard and nodded. "I want you to run there, and I'll be right behind you."

After hiking Ben higher in her arms, she took

off at a slow jog, mostly because she couldn't see more than a few feet in front of her face. She didn't realize she was holding her breath until her chest started to burn. She took a deep gulping breath and the tightness eased. After what seemed like forever, she reached the trees, darting behind them and sagging against a solid trunk.

Isaac joined her a few seconds later. "See anything?" she whispered.

He shook his head. "No, but we need to keep moving."

Of course they did. She sighed and pulled herself upright, shifting Ben to her other hip. Her arm muscles screamed in protest, but she forced herself to ignore the pain. Although maybe once this was all over, she'd have to start lifting weights so she wasn't so weak.

"I'd take him, but I need to cover your back," Isaac whispered, reading her thoughts.

"I'm fine." She made her way through the trees, grateful to see there was a clearing on the other side. She glanced up and noticed there was a church steeple not far away. "Isaac, can we go to that church up ahead?" she whispered.

"Sure, but keep to the shadows, in case they've figured out we've escaped."

Leah picked up her pace, despite her weary muscles. The church steeple was like a beacon, drawing her closer. She silently prayed as they made their way down the street, putting as much distance as possible between them and the American Lodge.

Leah wanted to cry with relief when the church loomed before her. Although as they approached the steps, it belatedly occurred to her that the doors were likely locked.

"Wait—I want you two to stay hidden over here," Isaac said, drawing her away from the front steps.

She didn't have the strength or the will to argue. She huddled down near the corner of the building with Ben on her lap, not even caring that her jeans were getting all muddy again.

Too afraid to close her eyes, she peered through the darkness, making sure there were no cars coming toward them. From this angle she couldn't see what Isaac was doing, but since she was fairly certain the church was locked up, it didn't matter. Maybe he was checking for a side entrance or something.

Cold from the ground seeped through her clothing, making her shiver. She thought she might be warmer if she stood back up, but struggling to her feet wasn't easy, especially with Ben's weight in her arms.

"Leah?" Isaac seemed to pop up out of nowhere. "Come on. Let's get inside."

Inside the church? She was surprised but grateful as Isaac supported her, his arm anchoring her waist. Once they were safely in, he closed the door behind them.

She sank into a pew and then carefully set Ben down beside her. Clasping her hands together, she bowed her head and prayed.

"Thank You for providing us shelter, Lord. And thank You for keeping us safe from harm. Please continue to guide us to safety. Amen."

Isaac listened to Leah's softly uttered prayer and couldn't help wondering if her faith really offered as much support as she claimed. She certainly seemed to pray a lot, although he couldn't blame her, since she'd also been in constant danger.

He scrubbed his hands over his face, mentally kicking himself for nearly getting them captured once again. They'd been found too easily.

But how?

He crossed over to where Leah sat and edged in beside her. "I'm sorry about this," he murmured. "I promise I'll do a better job of protecting you and Ben from here on."

Her attempt at a smile fell short, but he gave her points for trying. "It's not your fault, Isaac."

It was his fault, but there was no sense in hammering the issue any further. Looking backward wasn't going to help; they needed to move forward from here. "I talked to your brother earlier and he told me that he thinks there is a dirty cop involved in this mess."

Leah's face brightened. "You spoke to Shane? Is he okay?"

"He's hiding, but he's okay for now," Isaac confirmed.

"I'm so glad to hear that," she murmured. "I've been so worried about him."

"I know." Isaac put his arm around her shoulders and gave her a quick hug. "I have to think that whoever the shooter was at the side of the road somehow got the plate number for the police vehicle. The gunman likely didn't know that we had connecting rooms and simply tossed the gas canister into the one where the vehicle was parked." He was glad now that he hadn't left it in front of Leah and Ben's room.

"But how did they find us?" she asked.

"I wish I knew," Isaac admitted. "But it's obvious we need a vehicle with no ties to the SWAT team."

"Where on earth are we going to get another car?"

"Don't worry. Caleb and Deck will come through for us." Isaac hated to wake his buddies up again, especially at two in the morning, but what choice did he have? The church was a good sanctuary for now, but it was too close to the hotel for comfort. Once the person who'd thrown the tear gas realized they'd gotten away, they'd start to widen their search radius, and the church would become an obvious target.

At least, that was what he would do. And if a dirty cop was involved, he'd probably do the same thing.

Isaac pulled out his phone and called Deck. A few weeks ago, his buddy had been trying to sell his sister's old car. Maybe, just maybe, he hadn't sold it yet. The older-model vehicle would be perfect for them to use for a few days. And since Declan's sister had a different last name, it would be ideal.

Declan didn't answer right away, and when he finally did, he didn't sound too happy. "What?" he asked in a sleepy tone.

"I'm sorry, Deck, but we've been found. Someone threw a canister of tear gas into my hotel room. Do you still have your sister's old car?"

There was a long pause and Isaac hoped his buddy hadn't fallen back asleep. But when Deck spoke again, he sounded more awake. "Yeah, I still have it. Where are you and Leah now?"

"At the church located down the road from the hotel. If you could get here as soon as possible, we'd appreciate it."

"No problem. I'll have Bobby drive the spare car, since he's home on spring break."

"That works. If you could bring a computer, too, I'd appreciate it."

"A computer? Sure, I can loan you mine. What are you searching for?"

"Anything that explains what's going on," Isaac said, being purposefully vague. He didn't want to expose his friends to more danger. "Thanks, and I'm sorry to keep bothering you."

"You were there for me when I needed help, so it's no problem. We'll be there in fifteen to twenty minutes."

"We'll be waiting." Isaac disconnected the call, feeling better that they had a solid escape plan.

"Who's Bobby?" Leah asked.

She'd obviously heard the entire conversation—not a surprise, since she was sitting right next to him. So close he could smell the cinnamon scent that seemed to cling to her skin. "His brother-in-law."

"And you helped Declan out, the way he's helping you now?" she pressed.

He slowly nodded. "Yeah, about six months ago. We've always been there for each other no matter what."

"Mommy, I'm hungry," Ben said in a plaintive tone.

"I'm sorry, sweetie, but I don't have anything right now," Leah said, smoothing a hand over her son's hair. "Close your eyes and try to get some rest."

"We can stop and pick up something once we have a different set of wheels," Isaac offered.

"I think once he falls asleep, he'll be fine," Leah murmured.

"Yeah, well, all this running around is making me hungry, too," Isaac said in a wry tone as he rose to his feet. "Stay here. I'm going to make sure we're still in the clear."

He didn't really think they'd been followed, but he needed to put some distance between them. Leah's cinnamon-and-spice scent was wreaking havoc with his concentration. She was so beautiful, even after everything they'd been through, with her naturally curly black hair and heart-shaped face. There couldn't be anything but friendship between them, so why was he suddenly thinking of her as a woman he was attracted to?

He needed to get that thought out of his head right now. After pushing open the church door a crack, he peered outside. He couldn't see far, but what he did see seemed quiet and deserted.

Leah hadn't asked him how he'd gotten inside the church, and he was glad he didn't have to explain how he'd picked the lock. He couldn't help but think the church pastor wouldn't be too thrilled to know how easy it was to break in. Then again, maybe he should let the pastor know so he could change the locks.

But that would have to wait until they'd gotten safely out of this mess.

Waiting for Deck and Bobby to show up was agonizing, each second passing with excruciating slowness. Isaac paced back and forth, peering outside every so often.

Finally his phone rang, and he was relieved to see Deck's number. "Hey, are you close?"

"Yeah, we're parked in the back behind the church," Deck informed him. "Didn't see anyone suspicious hanging around, either."

"Thanks, Deck. We'll be outside soon." Isaac clicked off, then locked the main doors of the church before heading over to Leah and Ben. "They're here with the car, Leah. Do you want me to carry Ben?"

She looked dead on her feet, but still shook her head. "I'm worried he'll cry."

Isaac understood her concern, since there hadn't exactly been time to bond with the boy. Although he needed to spend more time with Ben so the boy wouldn't be afraid of him.

He led the way through the church to the back door. Leah followed slowly, carrying Ben, who was once again half-asleep.

There were two cars in the lot, both with their engines running but their lights off. Isaac stayed right beside Leah, sweeping his gaze over the area to verify they hadn't been found by the shooter.

As they approached the vehicles, a young man climbed out from behind the wheel of the older sedan and stepped forward. Isaac recognized Bobby Collins and gratefully took the keys he handed over.

"There's a booster seat in the back for the kid," Bobby said. "Figured that would be one less thing to worry about."

"Where did you get it?" Isaac asked in surprise.

"Caleb donated it," Declan said, coming out to join them. He handed Isaac a computer case. "Apparently his daughter, Kaitlin, had two of them."

"Thank you," Leah said with a tremulous smile.

"No problem." Bobby ducked his head shyly and sauntered over to the other car. Declan slapped Isaac on the back and then went to join his brother-in-law. Isaac waited for Leah to get Ben settled in the booster seat before he opened the front passenger door for her.

He didn't breathe easy until the church was far behind them. Isaac knew he needed to find another place to stay for what was left of the night, and this time he wasn't about to tell anyone, even his friends, where they were going.

Driving through the night, he finally came across a hotel that boasted two-bedroom suites.

The concept offered the best of both worlds, so he pulled in and parked.

Leah had been dozing and came awake in a rush when the car stopped. "Where are we?" she asked, rubbing her eyes.

"Brookside Suites Hotel," Isaac said. "They offer two-bedroom suites, so you and Ben can share one room and I'll use the other."

"Looks expensive," Leah murmured.

Isaac didn't answer, because he'd already had the same thought. But they couldn't afford to be cheap when it came to making sure they were safe. As it was, he'd need to convince the clerk to take cash when they were ready to check out.

It didn't take long to secure a room, although the man insisted on having a credit-card number on file in case there was any damage. Apparently Isaac's badge helped lend credibility, as the clerk reluctantly agreed to take payment in cash.

This time, Isaac carried Ben inside the hotel. The boy had fallen back asleep and barely stirred as they rode the elevator to the third floor. They had an inside room, and Isaac figured that they'd be much harder to find in a place like this, even if somehow the shooter figured out what kind of car they were driving, a nearly impossible feat.

Surely they'd be safe here.

Isaac waited for Leah to unlock the door and flip on the lights. The place was nice, as it should be for the price he'd paid. There was a comfortable living area, complete with a small kitchenette, so they could cook their own meals if they were going to stay for a few days.

The first bedroom had two double beds, and he waited while Leah pulled down the covers so he could set Ben down in the one nearest the bathroom.

She quickly stripped the boy's coat, hat mittens and boots off before covering him with the sheet and blanket. For a moment she simply stood there, staring down at her sleeping child. Isaac eased toward the door, thinking that maybe she wanted some privacy.

But she surprised him by turning and following him out to the living area. "It's hard to believe we're finally safe," she murmured, running a hand through her hair.

Isaac had to stop himself from wrapping her in his arms and holding her close. He cleared his throat and nodded. "No one knows we're here, Leah. The car can't be traced to us, either. We are safe."

Her smile was a tad pathetic, but still made his heart race. "I finally believe that."

He cleared his throat again, hoping she couldn't tell how nervous he was. "I'm going to go back down to get the laptop, okay?"

"Sounds good."

He left the room, thinking for sure Leah would be tucked in bed by the time he returned. He wouldn't blame her one bit, since he doubted she'd gotten much sleep before the tear-gas incident.

Grabbing the computer case out of the backseat didn't take long, and within minutes he was back upstairs, using his key card to access the room. When he opened the door, he was surprised to find Leah curled in a corner of the sofa, waiting for him.

She glanced over when he walked in. "Did you want me to order something to eat? You mentioned you were hungry."

Isaac was touched by her offer. When was the last time anyone cared about whether he was tired or hungry?

"Thanks for the thought, but I doubt they'll provide room service this late." He set the computer case down on the small table in the kitchenette.

"Really?" Leah seemed surprised and then shrugged. "You're probably right. It's closer to breakfast, anyway."

"Get some sleep, Leah," he suggested in a low tone. "I'm sure you're exhausted."

She dropped her gaze and nodded. "I am, but truthfully, I'm afraid I'll have nightmares."

The urge to offer comfort was strong. "I'm sorry," he murmured helplessly.

"It's okay." She uncurled herself from the sofa

and stood. To his surprise, she crossed over to him and put her hand on his arm. "Thanks for keeping us safe, Isaac." She stood on her tiptoes and brushed a kiss across his cheek before turning to head into her room.

It took every ounce of willpower he possessed to let her walk away, when all he really wanted to do was haul her close for a real kiss. He didn't let out his breath until she'd closed the door behind her, the cinnamon-and-spice scent lingering long after she'd gone.

He gave himself a stern talking-to as he headed into his room. He wasn't in the market for a relationship. And Hawk wouldn't appreciate knowing how much Isaac thought about kissing his sister.

From here on out, he needed to keep his distance from Leah. For both their sakes.

FIVE

Leah awoke with a start, to find bright sunlight streaming through the window. For a minute she couldn't figure out where she was, but then the events from the night before came rushing back to her.

The masked man, the Jeep sliding into a ditch, the canister of tear gas. She pushed her tangled hair away from her face, amazed that she'd slept so soundly after all that. When she glanced over at Ben's bed, her heart flew into her throat, because it was empty.

"Ben?" She leaped out of bed and dashed over to open the door. She needn't have worried, for Isaac had everything under control. He was seated beside Ben, the two of them enjoying a hearty meal of scrambled eggs and bacon.

"Good morning, Leah," Isaac said. "Are you hungry? I didn't order anything for you yet, because I didn't want the food to get cold."

"I— Um, yes. I'm hungry." She was glad to

see that Ben must be getting over his nervousness around Isaac. They looked quite cozy eating breakfast together.

"It will take a few minutes for them to deliver," Isaac said as he reached for the phone. "But I have coffee here if you want some."

"I'd love a cup." Leah crossed over and helped herself to a steaming mug. She doused it with cream and then carried it back to her room. If breakfast was going to be a while, she'd spend the time getting cleaned up.

She emerged from the bathroom twenty minutes later, feeling much better even though her mud-splattered jeans were beyond redemption. But she pulled them on anyway, because she didn't have anything else to wear.

Making a mental note to convince Isaac they needed to go shopping, she came out of the bedroom to the enticing aroma of bacon and eggs.

"Smells delicious," she said, pulling out a chair next to her son. At this moment it was almost as if none of the terrible things had happened last night.

"Trust me, it is." Isaac stood and moved his dirty dishes out of the way so she'd have more room.

"Mr. Isaac is a policeman just like Uncle Shane," Ben said, his eyes gleaming with excitement. "Isn't that cool?"

She forced a smile for Ben's sake. "You bet."

"Are we gonna see Uncle Shane soon?" he asked.

"I'm not sure. I think he's working," she hedged.

"He saves people, right, Mommy?" Ben persisted.

"Yes, he does. And so does Mr. Isaac."

"Ben, how about we let your mom eat her food before it gets cold?" Isaac suggested.

"Okay."

Leah gave Isaac a grateful smile and then bowed her head for a quick, silent prayer of thanks before digging into her breakfast. She had to admit the food was amazing, or maybe it was just that she was incredibly hungry.

Isaac went over to the sofa and began working on his computer.

"Can I watch cartoons, Mom?" Ben asked as he finished his eggs. "Please?"

"Sure," she said, glancing at Isaac. He smiled and picked up the remote, finding a children's channel without difficulty.

Ben abandoned his dirty dishes, running toward the sofa. Without a moment's hesitation, he climbed up and settled in beside Isaac.

For a moment Leah stared at the two of them sitting together, wishing for something she couldn't have. She gave herself a mental shake and concentrated on finishing her breakfast.

The sound of cartoons reminded her of Saturday mornings at home. Sometimes, if he happened to be off work, Shane would come and join them.

Thinking about her brother made her push her empty plate away with a heavy sigh. Here she was, enjoying a nice breakfast, while her brother was who knew where, fighting to stay alive. What was wrong with her?

Quickly, she cleared away the dirty dishes, stacking them on the tray and pushing it out into the hallway for the hotel staff to pick up.

"Isaac? Could you come over here for a minute?"

He looked surprised, but set his computer aside to stand.

"Please bring the laptop," she added.

Isaac's eyebrows rose, but he did as she requested, unplugging the cord and carrying everything over to the small table. "What's wrong?" he asked in a low voice.

"We have to do something to find Shane." She wasn't about to take no for an answer. "There must be something we can do to help him."

"I understand how difficult this must be for you," Isaac said. "But I offered to help your brother and all he asked was that I keep you and Ben safe."

"Yeah, but who's helping him?" she asked in

an exasperated tone. "We can't just sit here twid-
dling our thumbs. Shane admitted he's in trouble,
and we have to do something to help."

"Do you have any idea where to start?" Isaac
asked.

Her shoulders slumped in defeat. She didn't
have any clue where Shane might be. How could
she? Her chest ached with the sick realization that
it was her own fault. She'd allowed him to keep
the dangerous aspects of his job a secret. In fact,
she'd forced the issue, often changing the subject
if he brought up something that reminded her of
the way they'd lost their father.

Losing their dad had destroyed their family.
Her mother had turned to alcohol, Shane had gotten into trouble and she'd buried herself in her
studies, trying to block everything else out.

But no more hiding from reality. She drew in
a ragged breath. "There has to be something we
can do," she insisted. "What about Shane's partner? Trey Birchwood? Couldn't we try to find
him and talk to him?"

"That might be a good place to start," Isaac
agreed. "Hawk said not to trust him, but that
doesn't mean we can't ask him a few questions.
But first I have to find out what he looks like."

Leah sipped her coffee as Isaac punched the
computer keys, pulling up Trey's driver's license.

He spun the computer toward her so she could see the screen. "Does that look like him?"

She chewed her lower lip as she stared at the grainy photograph on the screen. "I only met him once, but I'm pretty sure that's him."

"All right, I'll take a drive past his place, see if he's around. When I called the Fifth District police station late last night, they said he was off work this weekend."

"Wait a minute. I want to go with you," she protested with a frown.

But Isaac was already shaking his head. "I can't put you and Ben in danger. I promised Hawk I'd keep you safe."

"I understand, and trust me, I want to keep Ben safe, too. But we also need to buy a few things, at least a change of clothes and something to help keep Ben entertained for a while, as I'm sure cartoons aren't going to hold his interest for long. Couldn't we go to one of those big-box stores? And maybe cruise past Trey Birchwood's house on the way?"

Isaac scowled, but glanced over at Ben, as if considering her idea. "I guess you're right," he admitted finally. "We should probably pick up a few things."

"I have some cash," she said, in case he was worried about how much she planned to spend. "And I have my debit card, too."

"Cash only," he said in a stern tone. "We don't want to leave an electronic trail."

She pursed her lips, mentally calculating how much she had on hand. Luckily, she'd gotten in the habit of carrying a small, secret stash of cash for emergencies, and this was definitely an emergency. "All right, no cards. When can we leave?"

Isaac hesitated. "Soon, since it's almost checkout time." Her disappointment must have shown, because he added, "I'm not sure if staying here another night is the right thing to do. I feel like we should keep moving, just in case."

She glanced around the cozy suite, wishing they could stay another day, but knowing that it was far too expensive. And besides, moving around was probably the smart thing to do.

"All right, that gives us roughly thirty minutes or so. Is there anything else we can search for on the laptop?"

"Mom, cartoons are over," Ben shouted. "Can we go swimming? Or find a playground?"

Isaac shut down the computer. "We're going shopping first, okay?"

"Shopping, yuck," the boy muttered with a pout.

"I thought maybe you'd like to get the new handheld video game that's out," Leah offered. "But if you'd rather not..."

"I do! I want it!" Ben's mood instantly did a three-sixty, making her smile.

Isaac chuckled, too. "All right, let's get going."

Leah ducked into the bathroom to gather up the toiletries and stuff them into her purse. She was desperate to wash her hair, but needed to purchase a brush first or her curly hair would be nothing but a snarled mess.

Ben and Isaac were waiting by the door when she returned, and they left together to walk down to the parking lot. The sky was overcast, but it wasn't raining, at least not yet, but it was windy. Tree branches swayed wildly as Isaac led the way to their car, which was good, since she couldn't remember much after they'd left the church. She made a mental note of the sedan's color and tag number.

"Stay here. I'll be right back after I check out," Isaac instructed.

She nodded, glad the car's heater was turned on high. Maybe it was the howling wind that made her feel chilled. Certainly there was no reason to be afraid.

"Where's Mr. Isaac?" Ben asked after two minutes had passed. "We need to hurry up and buy my game."

"He's paying for the room, and don't worry. We'll get to the store soon enough." Leah didn't like having to buy a video game for Ben, but clearly, the poor kid needed something to do in the endless string of hotel rooms.

She made a mental note to make sure the next place they stayed was near some playground equipment. Granted, the weather wasn't great, but it would still be good for Ben to spend some time outdoors.

There was a loud thud that caused her heart to leap into her throat. It took a minute for her to realize that a tree branch had broken loose and hit the side of the building.

Isaac returned, sliding into the driver's seat. As he glanced over at her, flashing a reassuring grin, she realized just how nice it was to have him beside her.

And she wondered if God had brought Isaac into her life for more than one reason. To keep her safe, yes, but maybe also to show him the way to faith and God?

If so, that was a mission she couldn't ignore.

Isaac wasn't fond of shopping, but he had to admit that poring over the various handheld video games with Ben was kind of fun. Isaac didn't know much about the various games, but it was clear the boy did.

Spending time like this was what he missed the most after losing Jeremy. Isaac treasured the memories he had and grieved for the ones he'd never have again.

While he and Ben spent time in the games department, Leah went off to find the clothing and toiletries she wanted. When she came back, he was surprised to find that she'd tossed in a few items for him, too.

"These might not be the correct size, so if you want to go try them on that's fine," she said, her cheeks pink with embarrassment.

He glanced at the tags and lifted a brow. "Good eye. These should fit fine."

She ducked her head and shrugged. "I simply bought the size that Shane wears," she murmured. "Did you find the video game you wanted?" she asked Ben.

"Yep. Me and Mr. Isaac picked this one," he said, waving it in front of her face. "But can I have the dinosaurs, too? Please?"

Isaac pulled the box of plastic dinosaurs off the shelf. "Sure you can," he said, placing it into the already-filled cart. He tried to figure out how much their bill would be and wondered if he should have hit Declan up for a loan.

Leah sent him an exasperated glance, but nodded. "Sure. Anything else? How about the toy cars?"

"Okay!" Ben's eyes were wide with excitement and Isaac couldn't help but grin in response. He barely remembered ever being as happy as Ben was, but then again, his home life hadn't been anything close to Ben's, either.

His dad had taken off when he was thirteen, and his mother had trailed a series of men through their apartment for the next few years. Isaac had often avoided going home, hanging out with his friends instead. Of course, that was exactly how he'd managed to get in trouble. And then arrested for selling drugs. It was a bad choice to make, doing something as drastic as selling drugs to get money for food, but at least he'd been given the chance to get back on track.

He shook off his thoughts, knowing this was hardly the time to take a stroll down memory lane. He wasn't the only kid with a rough up-bringing, and he certainly wouldn't be the last. And every year he made an anonymous donation to the Saint Jermaine boys' school, so that other kids would have the same chance to turn their lives around that he and Hawk had had.

Leah headed for the checkout line, and he followed more slowly, pulling out his wallet and counting how much cash he had. They couldn't afford to use everything, since they'd need to save some for the hotel they'd need to find later that night.

"Wait—what are you doing?" he asked when

Leah drew a stack of bills from the depths of her purse.

"Most of this is for me and Ben," she said, handing her money to the clerk.

"Don't spend all of it," Isaac protested. "Here, I'll pay for my stuff."

She reluctantly accepted his money, and he planned to call Deck for additional cash as soon as possible. Isaac had no idea how long they'd be on the run, but he knew it could easily be days, if not up to a week.

He grabbed the bags before she could and followed her and Ben back to the car. He stashed their purchases in the trunk, except for the video game, and then slid behind the wheel.

Leah opened the package and inserted the batteries before handing the game back to Ben. At least having it would give the poor kid something to do.

"Are we going to drive over to Trey's now?" she asked in a low voice.

"Yeah, we'll check things out," Isaac agreed. It was still early, just past one o'clock in the afternoon. Even if he wanted to get another hotel room, they wouldn't be able to check in for a couple of hours yet. Surely it couldn't hurt to drive over to Trey's apartment building and scope the place out?

He had the address plugged into the GPS on his phone, and Leah gave him directions.

"I think that's the place," she said excitedly after verifying with the GPS. "The middle white-and-black brick building."

He nodded. The four-family apartment building was nestled between two other similar ones. "We're looking for a dark blue Ford Taurus," he said as he pulled into the parking lot behind the place.

"I don't see it," Leah murmured.

He didn't, either, and the lot wasn't all that big, so he turned around and drove back out to the street, making another loop around the block.

"Now what?" Leah asked. "Should we wait here for a while?"

Isaac pulled over to the side of the road and drummed his fingers on the steering wheel. "I don't know," he said in a low voice. "We could be wasting our time. For all we know, Trey is out of town."

"I guess you're right," Leah murmured in a dejected tone. "But what else can we do to help Shane?"

Good question. Too bad he didn't have an equally good idea. They could sit here all day without seeing Trey at all. Was Trey helping Hawk? Or busy trying to set him up? Either way, Trey was really the only lead they had.

Isaac should have insisted that Hawk give him more to go on. He could try getting in touch with that ATF agent, Cameron Walker, but Hawk had specifically asked him not to do that.

Isaac was just about to pull away from the curb when he saw a dark blue car approaching. He straightened in his seat, peering through the windshield at the driver.

"Is that Trey?" Leah whispered.

"I think so." Sure enough, the car turned into the driveway of the apartment building. Isaac couldn't afford to let this opportunity to talk to Hawk's partner slide through his fingers, so he glanced at Leah. "Get behind the wheel and keep the car idling," he instructed. "I'm going to see if I can talk to Trey, but if anything happens, I want you to drive away, okay? Don't worry about me. Just make sure that you and Ben stay safe."

Her blue eyes were wide, but she nodded. "I understand."

He glanced up and down the street, making sure that no one was obviously watching him, before he slid out of the driver's-side door and ducked his head against the wind.

He'd parked down the street, hoping to blend in with some of the other cars that were parked there. He forced himself to adopt a leisurely pace as he headed toward the apartments. Isaac walked up the driveway, then paused by a large evergreen tree that towered next to the building.

Now that he was here, he tried to formulate in his mind exactly what he was going to say to Trey Birchwood. Hawk had told him not to trust anyone, but Isaac had to believe that Trey knew something about what his partner's undercover operation involved. He'd just have to play it by ear and hope Hawk's partner let something slip.

Not the best plan in the world, but good enough for now.

Isaac was about to make his way around the tree and down the driveway when a man came striding past, wearing a black leather jacket and a black ball cap pulled low over his face.

There was something familiar about the way the guy moved, and for a moment the image of the masked man lurking outside Leah and Ben's house flashed in Isaac's mind. He quickly lifted his phone and snapped a picture, even though he knew he wouldn't get a good view of the man's face. Isaac eased himself farther into the narrow space between the tree and the building, hoping he wouldn't be noticed hiding there.

But Isaac needn't have worried; the guy never looked back. Instead, he jumped into an SUV and drove away, thankfully in the opposite direction from where Leah and Ben were waiting.

Isaac had a bad feeling about what had just

happened, and he quickly rounded the tree and jogged to the parking lot. He saw Trey's vehicle in the back corner, and for a moment he thought the car was empty.

But as he drew closer, he realized that a figure was slumped over the steering wheel.

Isaac's gut tightened as he quickened his pace. Within moments he reached the driver's-side window of the blue car and peered inside.

A bullet hole in Trey's temple confirmed his worst suspicions.

Hawk's partner was dead.

And Isaac was pretty sure the guy in the black leather jacket, the same guy who'd tried to kidnap Leah and Ben, had killed him.

SIX

Leah gripped the steering wheel, craning her neck so that she could watch Isaac's progress as he crossed the street and then huddled behind the pine tree.

What on earth was he waiting for?

The tiny hairs on the nape of her neck lifted when she saw a man with a black leather jacket and cap stride down the driveway of the apartment building. She ducked her head, but he climbed into an SUV that was parked on the other side of the road.

As he drove away, she stared at his license plate, but caught only the first three letters, *CXF*. She repeated them over and over in her mind so that she wouldn't forget.

When she glanced at the pine tree, her stomach dropped when she realized Isaac wasn't there. She gripped the steering wheel harder, hoping nothing was wrong. Was she overreacting about seeing the man in the black jacket? Could it be that he lived in the building and for some reason hadn't bothered to park in the lot?

Behind her, Ben played his video game, oblivious to her racing thoughts. She toyed with the idea of driving off, the way Isaac had told her to. Except that nothing dangerous had happened, right?

So why did she feel this weird, impending sense of doom?

She craned her neck so that she had a good view of the driveway, but there was still no sign of Isaac. Leah gnawed her lower lip, worried about him. Surely he was safe in broad daylight?

It seemed like an hour later, but it was really only eight minutes before she caught a glimpse of him coming down the driveway. As he jogged toward the car, she pried her hands from the steering wheel and awkwardly crawled over the center console to the passenger seat.

He slid behind the wheel, his jaw set and his expression grim.

"What happened?" she asked as he put the car in gear and drove away. He didn't rush, but seemed to take his time as he made his way around the block.

Isaac glanced in the rearview mirror and she couldn't help swiveling in her seat to see for herself if someone was behind them. As far as she could tell, they weren't being followed.

"Did you get to talk to Trey?" she asked after several minutes had passed.

"No. Unfortunately, Trey Birchwood is dead."

"What?" Leah's jaw dropped in horror and she wondered if she'd heard him wrong. "But we saw him drive into the parking lot."

"The guy in the black jacket must have been waiting for him," Isaac murmured. "I should have flagged Trey down before he pulled in...."

"Wait a minute. That guy in the black leather jacket? The one who jumped into the SUV? That guy?"

Isaac glanced at her in surprise. "You saw him?"

She nodded. "Yeah, I saw him. I tried to get his license number, but only caught the first three letters, *CXF*. But I noticed what kind of car he was driving." She told him the brand.

Isaac raised his eyebrows and whistled. "Expensive car, but at least knowing that along with the first three letters of the plate number should help us track down the owner."

"Unless it's stolen," Leah said in a wry tone. "Then we're back to square one."

"Not exactly. I did find one other clue," Isaac said as he headed onto the interstate. She wanted to ask where they were going, but suspected he didn't have a specific destination in mind.

"Really?"

He nodded. "There was blood on the asphalt, likely seeping out from the driver's-side door, so I looked under the car and found a shell casing. It's not much, but it's better than nothing."

Leah frowned. "What can a shell casing tell us?"

For the first time since he'd come back to the car, Isaac smiled. "Believe me, a single shell casing can tell us more than you think. It can reflect the killer's signature, so to speak. Although having the bullet would be even better."

She'd take his word for it. "Shouldn't we call the police about Trey?"

"Yes, but we're not using our personal cell phones," Isaac said in a firm tone. "We can't risk anyone tracing us to the call. We'll find another of those big-box stores and buy a couple of prepaid cell phones, just in case."

Leah couldn't argue with his logic, and it wasn't as if a short delay would cause more harm to Trey. "Why do you think he was killed?"

Isaac let out a heavy sigh. "I wish I knew. Could be that Trey did set up your brother and had to be silenced because he was a loose end. Or it could be the exact opposite—that Trey was actually innocent and was killed because he wouldn't turn on his partner. Based on how they tried to get to you, I'm inclined to believe the latter."

Leah shivered and sent up a quick prayer for

Trey Birchwood, just in case he was nothing more than an innocent bystander.

She didn't say anything more until Isaac pulled into the parking lot of another big store. "We can wait here," she offered.

He nodded. "I'll be right back."

She watched him stride into the entrance and then leaned her forehead on the passenger-side window. It was two o'clock in the afternoon and she was already exhausted. How did Isaac do this sort of thing on a regular basis?

She had no idea, but it was clear she wasn't cut out for it. She refused to open her heart, only to get hurt again.

This wasn't the life she wanted. Not for herself and certainly not for Ben.

Isaac quickly purchased the prepaid phones and then made his way back to the car. As much as he wanted to make the call to the Fifth District police station right away, he needed to power up the devices and activate them before he could use them.

He slid behind the wheel and handed the bag containing the phones to Leah.

"Where should we go now?" she asked.

"It's just past two-thirty, but we might be able to find a place that will let us check in early." At least, he hoped so. The sooner he could call in Trey's murder, the better.

"Okay. We should probably pick up something to eat, too, since I'm sure Ben will be hungry."

Isaac nodded, having the same thought. It had been a long time since he'd had to worry about keeping on a schedule for the sake of a child. He headed west on the interstate, keeping a keen eye out for a suitable hotel, not caring that he was going farther and farther out of town. As far as he was concerned, the farther away from Trey's dead body, the better.

When he came across another hotel that offered suites, he exited the freeway and pulled into the parking lot.

The clerk was nice enough to give them the room right away. Isaac hauled in their shopping bags and then quickly charged up the prepaid phones.

Leah and Ben took their time going through all the purchases, and soon the boy had the dinosaurs spread out on the living room table. Isaac stared for a minute, remembering how much Jeremy had loved dinosaurs. The ache in his heart wasn't as bad as it used to be. He tore his gaze away with an effort and quickly activated the phones.

Thankfully, it didn't take long for the process to work, and he went out in the hallway to make his call to the police station.

It wasn't easy. The dispatcher pressed him for details, and eventually he simply hung up, knowing that while they might think he was some sort of crazy man, they'd still investigate the information he'd given them.

It bothered him that he'd taken the shell casing from the crime scene. Obviously, it was a key piece of evidence, one that the police would need to solve Trey Birchwood's murder. But if someone inside the Fifth District was dirty, Isaac couldn't afford to give up the only clue they had. At least not until he'd had a chance to put the information into their database.

He sat down in the stairwell for a moment, staring at the phone. Resolutely, he punched in Hawk's number, wishing he could talk to his friend about Trey's death. But he wasn't surprised to get a message saying the number was out of service.

That was the same message he'd gotten before, and eventually Hawk had called him back. Isaac stashed the disposable phone in his pocket and scrubbed his hands over his face. Trey's murder had brought an abrupt end to the only lead he had. So now what?

His priority was still to keep Leah and Ben safe, and being here in a different hotel in a different city was the first step in doing that. Just like Hawk, he knew they couldn't afford to stay in one place for long.

For a moment he felt as if the weight of the

world was on his shoulders. What if he messed up? He was fortunate that the killer hadn't seen Leah and Ben in the vehicle outside Trey's apartment building, or things could have ended much differently.

Isaac couldn't bear the thought of letting them down, the same way he had Becky and Jeremy.

"Isaac?"

He jerked his head up to find Leah standing behind him, a worried expression on her face.

"Are you all right?" she asked, her eyes full of concern.

He managed to stop himself from shaking his head. "Yeah. I just got off the phone with the police station. I'm sure they think I'm some sort of goofball, but I did tell them about Trey."

She nodded, then came to sit beside him. "You're not in this alone," she said in a low tone. "God is always with us, showing us the way. He'll keep us safe."

Isaac wasn't so sure he shared her belief, yet at the same time, he found himself hoping she was right. Because right now, he wouldn't mind a little help.

Praying wasn't his thing, but he figured God was probably watching over Leah and Ben. So he lifted his eyes upward and silently prayed, *Please keep Leah and Ben safe!*

The dread around his heart lightened. "We'd

better get back inside," he said, rising to his feet and holding out a hand to Leah. When she placed her small palm in his, an odd tingling sensation caught him off guard.

Was he losing his grip on reality? He sure hoped not.

"Ben found a children's movie on TV," Leah said as they walked back to the room. "But I think he's getting hungry."

"How about I order a pizza?" Isaac offered. "With everything that happened, we forgot to pick up something to go."

"Ben's favorite is pepperoni," she said with a smile. "If you want anything more adventurous, you better order half and half."

"What do you like on your pizza?" he asked. "I'd rather make sure you get what you like, too."

Her cheeks went pink again and she shrugged. "I love just about anything except anchovies."

A woman after his own heart. "I'm not fond of the little fishes, either, so how about I get a medium pizza with the works for us and a small pepperoni for Ben?"

"That's great, if you think we can afford it," she said as she used her key to open the door.

"I have plenty of money," he assured her. "I just need Declan to bring me more cash."

"I have money, too," she pointed out. "Just so we're clear."

He could tell she didn't want to be indebted to him, and for some reason that made him upset. She and Ben were innocent bystanders in all this. She shouldn't have to use her own money to keep herself safe.

But there would be plenty of time to argue about money later. Right now, his growling stomach propelled him to the hotel phone, where he quickly placed their pizza order.

After he finished, he crossed over to the kitchen table, where Leah was sitting in front of the laptop. "What are you looking for?" he asked, dropping into the chair beside her.

"I was trying to find that website you used earlier, to see if I could plug in the first three letters of that license plate," she admitted.

"You won't have the same access I have." Isaac turned the computer so that he could access the secure website that allowed him to search license-plate numbers.

"What were those three letters again?" he asked.

"CXF," she answered, hovering near his shoulder, her nearness a definite distraction.

He tried to ignore his awareness of her as he typed in the partial plate and the make and model of the vehicle before hitting the search key. There were literally dozens of possibilities, but soon he was able to weed them down to three likely candidates.

"Write these names down," Isaac said. "I'll ask Caleb and Declan to run them through the system. Maybe we'll get a hit."

"All right," Leah agreed. "Although none of the names sound familiar."

"I know. I was hoping one would ring a bell with me, too. But don't forget your theory that the car could be stolen."

Leah grimaced. "I hope not."

He eased his chair away, wishing the pizza would hurry up and get there. Leah's scent was driving him crazy and he knew better than to get tangled up with a woman who made it clear she didn't date cops. Which was probably for the best, since he wasn't ready to get emotionally involved with a woman anyway.

As soon as they finished eating, he planned to ask Caleb or Declan to come out with more cash and to pick up the shell casing. Right now, that casing was the best clue they had, and he was anxious to get moving on it.

The phone rang and he leaped at the chance to put more distance between him and Leah. "Hello?"

"There's a pizza delivery here for room 2204."

"I'll be right down." He hung up the phone and glanced at Leah. "Our food is here. I'll be right back. Don't open the door for anyone but me."

She nodded and he left to go down to the lobby,

feeling a little foolish for being so paranoid. But the image of Trey's dead body seemed to be permanently ingrained on his mind.

By the time he arrived back in the suite, Leah had cleared off the small table and somehow managed to pry Ben away from his movie. Isaac set the boxes down and opened the tops.

"Yummy! I'm starving," Ben said, obviously anxious to start eating.

"Wait—we have to pray first, remember?" Leah captured her son's hand before he could grab for a piece of pizza. "Besides, it's probably hot."

Isaac hid a smile as he settled into the empty chair on the other side of Ben, who put his tiny palms together and bowed his head.

Isaac followed the child's example, waiting for Leah to begin her prayer.

"Dear Lord, we thank You for providing this wonderful food for us and for keeping us safe for another day. We also ask You to guide Shane home, keeping him safe from harm. And lastly we ask You to have mercy on Trey Birchwood's soul. Amen."

"Amen," Ben echoed.

"Amen," Isaac added. He felt Leah's surprised gaze rest on him, but in a flash the poignant moment was gone as she served Ben a slice of pizza.

Sharing a meal with them was nice, even if it reminded him of what he'd lost. The memories of the past weren't strong enough to diminish the reality of the present, and for the first time in the two years since Jeremy had died, Isaac found a measure of peace in the idea that maybe, just maybe, his son's soul was safe in God's care, too.

"Are you all right?" Leah asked, dragging him from his thoughts.

"Yeah, fine." He forced a smile, not sure she'd appreciate the fact that he was thinking about how nice it must be to have a family. Of course, normally Hawk would be here, instead of him.

"Vroom, vroom," Ben said before taking a big bite out of his pizza.

"Ben, please stop playing with your food," she said in a stern voice.

"I'm not playing. My pizza is a real car," Ben pointed out with logic that only another five-year-old would understand. "Vroom."

Leah sighed and glanced at Isaac as if looking for support. "Ben, you heard your mother," he said. "Finish your pizza, or if you're already full, then go wash up."

For a moment Ben stared at him, as if debating whether or not to listen, but then he popped the last bit of pizza into his mouth and reached for a napkin. "All done," he announced, through a mouthful of food.

"Go wash up in the bathroom, Ben," Leah said. She stood and began cleaning up the mess.

"Let's save the leftovers for later," Isaac suggested, putting all the pizza onto one plate. "After all, we may as well put the fridge to good use."

"Sounds like a plan."

Once the kitchen table was cleared, Ben came scampering back, putting his arms around Leah's waist. "Will you play dinosaurs with me? Puleeze?"

"Sure." She took him over to where the dinosaurs were scattered, and soon they were both making growling animal noises. Had Becky ever done that with Jeremy? Not that Isaac could remember. Then again, he'd usually picked up all the overtime he was offered, to help pay for all the nice things Becky liked to buy.

Shaking his head, he booted up his computer. There was something familiar about the guy he'd seen leaving the parking lot of Trey's apartment building, so he thought he'd start with doing a search on some of the kids he remembered from Saint Jermaine's. It wasn't easy—not just because eleven years had passed, but because they'd all had nicknames back then. It took a while to remember their real names.

Isaac searched a few, but didn't hit anything significant until he typed in *Wade Sharkey*. Wade's nickname had been Shark back then, and he'd picked a fight with Isaac, right after Isaac had gotten there, waving the tiny knife in his face.

Wade had a lot of friends back then, and they'd all ganged up against Isaac until Hawk had shown up, defusing the situation. Wade had made a couple of other attempts to get even with Isaac, punching him in the kidney when no one was looking, and one night he'd sneaked into Isaac's room and tried to suffocate him with a pillow. Once again, Hawk had saved him and tossed Wade out on his ear.

From that point on, there had been an uneasy truce between them. Isaac couldn't deny that he'd watched his back often, but about six months later, Wade had been sent back home.

Isaac stared at the adult photograph of Wade Sharkey, a mug shot taken about three years ago. Clearly, Wade hadn't turned his life around after leaving Saint Jermaine's. Instead, he'd done a stint in jail for armed robbery.

"Did you find something?" Leah asked, coming over to sit beside him.

He gestured to the computer screen. "Not really. This is just one of the kids your brother and I knew back at Saint Jermaine's."

Leah sucked in a harsh breath and Isaac frowned. "What is it? You recognize him?"

She slowly nodded. "He went to our high school. He was three years older than me, in Shane's class."

Isaac scowled. "You're saying he was friends with your brother?"

She shrugged. "They hung out together some-times, and he came to our house once. I remember, because I gave him a black eye when he forcefully tried to kiss me."

A flash of anger hit hard and Isaac had to take a couple of deep breaths to fight it back. Ridiculous to want to give Wade another black eye for something he'd done years ago.

"I bet Wade is part of the illegal arms dealing," he said in a low voice. "And that's why the ATF asked for your brother's help. Your brother was probably the best chance they had for getting close to Wade."

"Wade was a scary guy," Leah admitted in a low tone. "At least, back in high school, he scared me."

Isaac took her hand and gave it a reassuring squeeze. "I know, but don't worry. I'm not about to let him anywhere near you."

She tightened her fingers around his, and as he stared at their joined hands, he silently vowed to keep his promise.

Or die trying.

SEVEN

Leah clung to Isaac's hand and did her best to tear her gaze away from the disturbing image of Wade Sharkey on the laptop screen. He'd tried to kiss her, but she'd managed to get away before he could do anything more.

"Do you think he's involved in whatever Shane was investigating?" she asked, meeting Isaac's troubled gaze. "I wouldn't put it past him to do something criminal."

"Yeah, I think he's involved," Isaac admitted. "But try not to worry about this, Leah. He's not going to lay a finger on you as long as I'm here."

His words warmed her heart, and once again she realized how nice it was to have Isaac here, protecting her and Ben. Elliot would have tried to protect them, too, but he hadn't had the training Isaac did. Was she really comparing her husband to Isaac? What was she thinking? She cleared her throat and nodded. "I know. And right now, I'm more concerned about my brother." She shook her head helplessly. "Wade isn't the type of guy you want as your enemy."

"I agree," Isaac muttered. "He tried to kill me back at Saint Jermaine's, and Hawk saved my life. I'm not sure what your brother did to win him over, but from that point on he never tried to hurt me again. And I never did find out why Shark had it out for me in the first place."

"Shark?" she echoed in confusion before she made the connection. Wade's last name was Sharkey. "Oh, is that another of those nicknames you guys used back then?"

Isaac nodded. "Yeah."

"Unfortunately, that one suits him." Leah took a deep breath and forced a smile. "I guess the good news is that we have another clue." She subtly tugged her hand from his and then immediately missed his warm, comforting touch.

Isaac scowled. "But this clue doesn't help me much. Wade isn't going to be an easy man to find."

Her stomach twisted with fear. "You're not going to try to do that, are you?"

"I have to do something to help your brother, but I won't leave you here alone. I'll get Declan or Caleb to come and stay with you and Ben."

She wanted to protest, because truthfully, she'd be far more comfortable with Isaac. Yet shouldn't one cop be similar to another? It wasn't as if Caleb and Declan were complete strangers; she'd met them before.

Yet she wanted to be with Isaac instead of his teammates. Because he made her feel safe in a way no one else did.

Despite her best efforts to keep her distance, she realized she was beginning to get emotionally involved with Isaac Morrison. But she couldn't afford to let down her guard. That was a path that would only lead to emotional destruction.

Getting over Elliot's death had been hard enough. Especially since she'd had Ben, barely more than a baby at the time, to consider. She couldn't do it again. She couldn't afford to take the chance that she'd end up like her mother, broken and seeking solace in the bottom of a bottle.

Leah drew in a steadying breath. A relationship with any man, especially Isaac, was out of the question. For now they were forced to work together, because Shane needed help. So what if she was attracted to Isaac? She'd just have to get over it.

She forced herself to meet Isaac's gaze. "I'll be fine with Caleb or Declan," she agreed reluctantly. "But please be careful."

Isaac's smile was crooked. "I always am," he assured her.

Leah remembered her father saying the same thing, but in the end, all the caution in the world hadn't kept him safe.

But Elliot hadn't been safe, either.

She'd do her best to put Isaac's fate in the hands of God. And continue to pray for his safety.

That was as much as she'd allow herself to do.

Isaac could tell Leah was worried, and he wished there was a way he could assure her that everything would be fine.

He rose to his feet and pulled out his phone. Declan didn't answer, so he left a message. Thankfully, Caleb picked up.

"Hey, Caleb," Isaac greeted him. "I need a favor."

"Figured as much," his friend drawled. "What's up?"

"First of all, I need cash. You know I'm good for it."

"No problem," Caleb agreed easily. "How much?"

Isaac named an amount and was glad when his teammate didn't seem too shocked. Then again, both Caleb and Declan knew what it was like to stay hidden without leaving an electronic trail. Isaac had been there to help them, the same way they were assisting him now.

It was good to have friends who covered your back.

"Okay, what else?" Caleb asked.

This was the tricky part. "I need you to stay

with Leah and Ben for a while so I can do some legwork."

"Do you need help with the legwork, too?" Caleb asked. "I'll track down Deck."

"I already left him a message, so he might not be available. I can handle it alone, no worries," Isaac assured him. "There's a number of things we need to follow up on, three license-plate numbers that could belong to the guy who tried to snatch Leah and Ben. I also have a shell casing from a crime scene that I'd like you to run through the lab."

"Quite the list of favors," Caleb said drily. "Anything else?"

"Yeah, I want to know everything there is to know about ex-con Wade Sharkey."

"Who?" Caleb's tone held confusion.

"Check him out. He did time for armed robbery and is likely involved in the attempt to get to Leah and Ben."

Isaac could hear the tapping of computer keys in the background and wasn't surprised when Caleb let out a low whistle. "Yeah, I found him, and I'll see what we can dig up about his more recent activities. When do you want me to come over to sit with Leah and Ben?"

Isaac glanced at the clock and winced. "We've eaten an early dinner, but I'm sure you want to have dinner with your family, so maybe as soon as you're finished?"

"I'll come right away. Kaitlin and Noelle can eat without me."

That gave Isaac an idea. "You could eat dinner with your family and then bring them along. There's a pool here if Kaitlin likes to swim. I'm sure Ben wouldn't mind having a playmate."

"Great idea," Caleb agreed. "Kaitlin would love that. Tell me where you are again?"

Isaac gave the address and then disconnected from the call. He glanced at Leah, realizing she'd been listening to his side of the conversation. "I guess I should have run those plans by you first, huh?"

She shrugged. "No, it's fine. There's a shopping mall across the street, and we can pick up some swimming gear there. Ben will be ecstatic."

Isaac was glad she wasn't upset, but he could tell something was still bothering her. "Let's walk over now, okay? I want to be ready to leave as soon as Caleb gets here."

Leah pulled on her coat and helped get Ben into his. She was unusually quiet as they walked over to the discount store to buy swimsuits. It didn't take long, and within twenty minutes they were back in the hotel room.

Isaac jotted down some notes on Wade's last known address before shutting off the computer.

It was located within the Fifth District, which only made him more convinced that Wade was part of the illegal gunrunning. The address also happened to be smack-dab in the middle of one of the highest crime areas of the county, a fact Isaac purposefully didn't mention to Leah.

No sense in making her even more worried than she already was.

Isaac understood that she couldn't help thinking about her father's death on the job. It was a fate every cop on the force faced, although thankfully, deaths weren't as common anymore. The force put more time and effort into training, and the newest version of body armor also helped.

But he couldn't deny the risk and logically understood Leah's reluctance to be in that kind of position again, especially since she had Ben to worry about. After all, hadn't Isaac's job ruined his first marriage?

It had.

Too bad he couldn't seem to pry Leah out of his mind.

Leah was happy to see that Caleb had brought his wife, Noelle, along with their daughter. Kaitlin was a year or so older than Ben, but they seemed to get along fine.

Leah sat in a deck chair beside Noelle while Caleb joined the kids in the pool. She had to smile as the children splashed and tried to dunk him, which of course wasn't happening. Thankfully, Ben had taken swimming lessons, so she was comfortable watching from the side of the pool.

"Caleb certainly is great with kids," Leah said.

Noelle smiled and nodded, patting her slightly rounded stomach. "He's a wonderful father. And we're expecting another baby in about five months."

"Really? Congratulations!" Leah remembered how excited she and Elliot had been when she'd found out she was pregnant. "How is Kaitlin handling the news?"

"She's excited, too. I think she'll be a great big sister."

"I'm sure she will be," Leah agreed. She gave Noelle credit not just for being married to a cop—a member of the SWAT team, no less—but also having a family. "How do you handle it?" she asked. At the other woman's confused expression, she added, "You know, living with the stress of Caleb's job."

"It isn't easy," Noelle agreed. "But I don't sit by the radio like some of the cops' wives do. I teach preschool, so that tends to keep me busy."

"But don't you worry about him getting hurt?" Her expression turned serious.

"Sure, I worry about him. What cop's wife doesn't worry about her loved ones? But I have faith and pray every day that God will watch over Caleb."

Leah nodded, feeling a little ashamed that she'd even broached the subject. "Faith helps us get through all the difficult times, doesn't it?"

"Absolutely," Noelle agreed. "Look, you're in danger right now, and I'm sure that isn't because of anything you did, right?"

Leah let out a small laugh. "I'm a nurse—not exactly a dangerous job."

"Exactly my point. There are no guarantees for any of us. But I am glad that Isaac has been able to be there for you and Ben. He's a great guy."

If Noelle was trying to set her up with Isaac, she was on the wrong path. "I feel bad that you had to come out here to babysit me," Leah said, changing the subject. "I'm sure you had better things to do on a Saturday night."

"Are you kidding? I was thrilled at the chance of getting out of the house to bring Kaitlin to an indoor pool. And I'm sure your son is glad to have a playmate for a while."

"He is." She fell silent, watching the way Ben blossomed beneath Caleb's attention. Shane had been trying to fill the role of father figure for her son, but no matter how hard her brother tried, he couldn't be there as often as Ben needed.

And what would happen if her brother found someone to share his life with? Oh, Shane wouldn't abandon Ben completely, but she couldn't fault him for spending time with his own family.

Avoiding relationships hadn't been a conscious decision in the beginning, not during the first year or so after Elliot's death. If not for Ben, Leah wasn't sure she'd have found a way to get past her grief. There was a part of her that wanted to give up the way her mother had. Thankfully, the other part of her was just as determined not to.

But in the past two years she'd had several men ask her out, a couple of doctors at work and a construction worker from her parish. She hadn't been interested in going out with them, despite their so-called safe careers.

So why was she so attracted to Isaac? A man who was absolutely wrong for her on so many levels?

Maybe she needed to have her head examined. This was likely nothing more than a silly infatuation that would surely go away once her life went back to normal.

And if it didn't, she had only herself to blame.

Isaac avoided the freeway, taking a winding route along several side streets to get to the general area of Wade's last known address.

He was glad he was driving Deck's old car, since anything nicer would have been way out of place among the graffiti-painted buildings with boarded-up windows. Several cars around him had music blaring from the speakers, loud enough to be heard several feet away.

It would have been nice if Deck had been able to come with him, but unfortunately, he'd been out working on a suspicious device left at a shopping mall. And Isaac needed Caleb to stay with Leah and Ben.

Isaac wasn't foolish; he wasn't about to recklessly confront Wade, especially if he was surrounded by his buddies. He needed to get Shark alone, using their connected past to see if Wade knew anything about Hawk.

Finding the address wasn't difficult, but the apartment building looked to be deserted. Based on its dilapidated appearance, he figured it might even be condemned. For all he knew, Wade had moved someplace else.

Isaac referred to his notes, but didn't see the black car that, according to the DMV, was registered to Wade. Then again, the plates hadn't been renewed for the past two years, so the guy could be driving anything.

Isaac let out a sigh of frustration. Driving down here might be nothing but a bust. What had made him think he'd actually run into Wade? Especially on a chilly March evening?

Despite the cool temperatures, there were a few people out and about, and one particular group caught his eye. Even from a distance he could tell a drug deal was going down. But he wasn't here to worry about that. He needed to find Wade.

He passed a liquor store and caught a glimpse of another small group of guys inside. One of them looked familiar. He decided to park his car and continue on foot, to get closer.

Thankfully, he'd changed into the dark clothing Leah had picked out for him, black jeans and a sweatshirt, so he blended easily into the night. Most of the streetlights were burned out or broken, and it took a minute for his eyes to adjust to the darkness. The wind was cold and he pulled the hood of his sweatshirt over his head before making his way back to the liquor store.

He had no intention of going inside, just needed to get close enough to the glass door to see what was going on.

Walking slowly, Isaac tried to blend in with the rough neighborhood as he glanced into the liquor store. He caught a glimpse of a gun and a roll of cash exchanging hands. Satisfaction surged as his hunch proved correct.

The liquor store was being used as a hub for the sale of illegal weapons.

At that moment, the guy taking the money glanced over and locked gazes with Isaac. Not Wade, but another guy he recognized from Saint Jermaine's, one of Wade's sidekicks.

Isaac tore his eyes away and hunched his shoulders as he headed on around the block, taking the long way back to where he'd left his car. Every instinct screamed to run, but he forced himself to take his time, just in case the guy from Saint Jermaine's hadn't recognized him. He tried not to look too guilty as he rounded the corner.

A wave of relief hit hard when he reached his vehicle. Isaac found himself silently praying as he revved up the engine and pulled away from the curb. He had little choice but to drive past the liquor store, since there wasn't a cross street and making a U-turn would only cause more unwanted attention.

His brief moment of relief faded when he saw the guy he'd locked gazes with standing in the street facing him. As he approached, the man lifted his gun and pointed it directly at him.

Isaac cranked the steering wheel and ducked to avoid being hit as the sound of gunfire echoed through the night. He stomped on the accelerator, nearly clipping a parked car as he avoided the gunman in a desperate attempt to get back to Leah and Ben.

EIGHT

Leah couldn't seem to relax as the hours crept by. She put up a good front, laughing when Ben did a cannonball that managed to splash the adults sitting a good two feet from the edge of the pool and chatting with Noelle as if she didn't have a care in the world.

But she watched the clock, nerves stretched thin.

When Noelle declared it was time to get out of the water, Leah didn't protest. When Ben did another cannonball rather than getting out the way she'd told him to, she narrowed her gaze and glared at him.

"Now, Ben." She didn't have to use her stern tone often, but her son was clearly trying to show off for his new friend, Kaitlin.

But of course, Kaitlin wasn't even paying attention to him; she was huddled up in a large towel, being dried off by Noelle. Caleb had also gotten out of the water to grab a towel, and without anyone else in the pool, Ben didn't have a reason to stay.

He reluctantly climbed out and came toward Leah. She wrapped him in a towel and held him close. "I hope you had fun," she said as she helped dry him off.

He nodded vigorously. "Lotsa fun!"

"Good. I'm glad." She was happy that he'd been able to relax and play for a few hours. He was the innocent victim in all this.

She glanced at the clock again, to find it was only ten minutes past the last time she'd looked, and she tried not to worry. Whatever he was doing was taking Isaac a long time. Truthfully, she'd expected him back by now.

"Why don't we go back up to our suite so the kids can watch a movie?" she suggested, pasting a happy smile on her face. She felt bad that Caleb couldn't leave until Isaac returned.

"Which movie?" Kaitlin asked eagerly.

Leah racked her brain to come up with the title of the latest children's film that had recently been released on DVD. "You and Ben can pick," she said. "There are a couple of movies on demand that are available."

"Sounds good," Noelle agreed. "And I'll make some microwave popcorn."

Leah led the way up to the suite, using her key card to enter before holding the door for the others. She and Noelle insisted the kids change into dry clothes, which they did in record time. Within minutes the pair had picked a movie and were settled on the sofa with a bag of microwave popcorn. Leah was impressed that Noelle had come prepared with snacks.

Caleb had taken a seat at the table and was working on the laptop computer. Since Noelle seemed content to watch the movie, Leah crossed over to sit beside him.

"What are you looking for?" she asked.

"Isaac asked me to check into a couple of things," he said without looking up.

She leaned forward and saw that he was doing a search on Wade Sharkey. A chill snaked down her back and she hated the idea that Isaac was out there looking for him.

After about fifteen minutes, Caleb sat back with a sigh. "There isn't much out there on this guy. He sure knows how to fly under the radar."

That news was not reassuring. "We have names and addresses for owners of these three license plates," she said, holding out the notes. "One of them was possibly involved in the attempt to kidnap me."

"Hmm…" Caleb drew them closer and began entering the information into the computer. She didn't have access to police databases the way he did, and they had only the one computer, so there wasn't much she could do except watch.

Isaac's teammate frowned as he stared at the screen, and her stomach tightened. "What is it? Did you find something?"

"One of these cars belongs to a cop, but he reported it stolen," Caleb admitted. "Cop's name is Aaron Winslow."

Her pulse jumped at the news. "He must be the dirty cop that my brother mentioned."

Caleb grimaced and shook his head. "Hold on—we can't jump to conclusions, Leah. First of all, I've already checked, and Winslow isn't in the same district as your brother. And even then, if someone wanted to throw suspicion on a cop, the best thing to do is to steal their vehicle to use in a crime."

He had a good point. "Okay, but don't you think it's a bit of a coincidence that my brother thinks there's a dirty cop who blew his cover, and it just so happens that a cop's car is stolen to commit a crime? I'm not sure I buy that."

"Maybe, maybe not," Caleb murmured. "But if we could find something else to link this cop to the crime, then I'd be convinced."

Leah wasn't sure how on earth they'd manage to do that, but before she could ask anything more, she heard the door open. Isaac was back!

She leaped from her seat, knocking it over backward in her haste.

"Whoa, take it easy," Caleb said with a smile, righting the chair as she crossed over to Isaac.

"Are you all right?" she asked, raking her gaze over him, searching for blood.

"I'm fine," he assured her, reaching out to give her a brief hug. The gesture was so quick she couldn't help but wonder if she'd imagined it.

"Well?" Caleb asked. "Did you find anything?"

Isaac stepped back and nodded. "I think I stumbled across a place where they're doing some of their gun deals," he admitted. "Do you have a minute, Caleb? I want to show you something."

"Sure," he said easily. He crossed over and planted a kiss on the top of his wife's head. "Be right back," he assured her.

Leah wasn't about to be left behind, so she followed them out the door.

"Uh, why don't you wait here?" Isaac stopped in the hall, clearly not wanting her to tag along. "We'll be back in a few minutes."

What was with the sudden secrecy? She suppressed a sting of hurt. She didn't like the way Isaac was trying to put her off and had no intention of sitting around and waiting for him. She squared her shoulders and tucked a stray curl behind her ear. "No way. I'm coming with you."

Isaac stared at her for a long moment, a flash of

helplessness, or maybe it was frustration, darkening his features before he threw his hands in the air. "Fine, suit yourself."

"I will." She trailed behind the two men, her stomach twisting with every step. When they walked outside, she hugged herself as the wind whipped around them.

Caleb let out a low whistle and she shoved her hair out of her eyes, trying to figure out what was wrong. Had Isaac cracked up the car?

But then she saw it—a small hole in the center of the windshield. And she knew without being told that it had been made by a bullet.

Someone had taken a shot at Isaac.

And looking at the placement of the hole, she knew it was a minor miracle that he hadn't been injured or killed.

Isaac watched Leah go pale and wished she would have listened to him and stayed inside. He'd wanted to spare her the fear and horror that now shadowed her eyes.

"We'd better call a glass company in to get that repaired," Caleb said. "Driving around with a bullet hole in your windshield is a good way to get pulled over."

"Yeah, no kidding. But that wasn't why I asked you to come out here. There's a slug in the passenger seat. We need to pry it out and see if it matches any other crimes."

Isaac opened the passenger door and crawled inside. The bullet had struck the outer edge of the seat, closest to the driver's side. Six inches nearer and he would have been hit.

Swerving had saved his life, since he wasn't wearing body armor beneath his sweatshirt. Something he definitely should have considered, based on his plan to skulk around in the district with the highest crime rate.

He pushed the thought aside and used his pen-knife to widen the opening around the slug.

"It's jammed in there pretty good," he muttered.

"Do you need help?" Caleb asked.

"Nah, just give me a few minutes." He widened the hole until he could see all the way down to the wooden frame. Finally, he caught a glimpse of the slug embedded inside. He wasn't sure he'd be able to get it out using only his pocketknife, since the tweezers that came with it weren't superstrong.

He didn't want to add any marks to the bullet fragment, so he stopped and backed out of the car. "We're going to need a field kit to get that out," he said.

"I might have one in my car," Caleb stated, heading off to where he'd parked.

Isaac turned toward Leah, searching for something to say, but she was already walking away, heading back inside the hotel.

Somehow, he didn't think she'd gone in just because she was cold.

He knew that seeing the hole in the windshield and knowing there was a bullet fragment in the seat cushion had only proved to her just how dangerous his job was.

A sense of loss hit hard and he tried not to rub the ache in his chest. Stupid to feel bad about this, since he'd known all along that a relationship between them was out of the question.

Besides, he wasn't ready to have another family. What if he messed up again? And even if he was interested, Leah would never date a cop.

Better for his brain to get the message sooner rather than later.

"Here, let me try," Caleb said after he'd returned with the kit. He nudged Isaac aside and climbed into the passenger seat. It didn't take long with the proper equipment, and soon Caleb had the bullet fragment tucked into a small evidence bag.

"Not sure we'll get much off this," he said doubtfully. "It's pretty smashed up."

"Yeah, the shot came from close range. I was hoping the seat cushion may have protected it some."

Caleb shrugged. "It's still worth a try. I'll get this and the shell casing in tomorrow morning."

Isaac forced a smile. "Thanks. I appreciate your help. Especially coming over here tonight to stay with Leah and Ben."

Caleb waved him off. "It's nothing. Trust me, Kaitlin had a great time, and Noelle didn't mind getting out of the house for a while. But we'd better head home." His buddy cocked his head to the side. "Are you going to be all right here with Leah?"

"Why wouldn't I be? She's upset, but she'll get over it eventually." He almost winced at his own offhand comment. As if he didn't care about what Leah was going through.

Caleb snorted and shook his head. "You can't fool me, bro. I've been there and I know when a man is getting emotionally tangled with a woman. And you are definitely getting twisted up with that one."

"I don't plan on getting married again. One failure was enough for me. Besides, I get the feeling that Leah doesn't date cops. So whatever you think you're seeing is nothing more than your overactive imagination." Isaac slammed the car door with more force than was necessary. "Let's go get the rest of your family. And if you could call a glass company to come fix the hole, I'd appreciate it. I'd phone them myself but they'd ask for a credit card."

"I'll cover it, no problem."

Isaac led the way inside, surprised to find Leah chatting with Noelle as if she didn't have a care in the world.

Why he was bothered by that, he had no idea. He pulled out his phone, intending to call Leah's brother, when he remembered the photos he'd taken.

"Caleb, wait. Before you leave, take a look at these pictures." Isaac plugged his phone into the computer and downloaded the few he'd taken of the men standing on the street corner. "What do you think? Do any of these guys look familiar?"

His buddy squinted at the grainy pictures before shaking his head. "Not really."

"What about this one here?" Isaac had managed to get a decent profile shot of a guy standing inside the liquor store, the same one he'd recognized from Saint Jermaine's.

The one who'd shot at him without so much as blinking an eye.

"Sorry, man, he doesn't look familiar at all."

Isaac nodded. "Okay, just thought I'd check." He knew Hawk would remember him. Would likely even remember his name. This guy wasn't on the list he'd dredged up from his memory earlier.

But the shooter must be working with Wade. Isaac couldn't believe the tie back to Saint Jermaine's was nothing more than a coincidence.

"Okay. Thanks anyway." Isaac knew he needed to set up a meeting with Hawk. But that was easier said than done. His buddy didn't answer his phone or call very often.

"Movie's over," Leah announced. "Time to get ready for bed."

"No! I don't wanna go to bed." Ben thrust his lower lip out stubbornly. "Me and Kaitlin want to have a sleepover."

Isaac hid a smile as Leah stared at her son with exasperation.

"No sleepovers," Noelle said firmly. "Kaitlin, say thank you to Mrs. Nichols and Ben for inviting us to come and swim in the pool."

"Thank you, Mrs. Nichols and Ben," Kaitlin parroted. "I had lots of fun."

"Me, too," Ben declared, unwilling to be left out. "Mom, can Kaitlin come back tomorrow?"

"We'll see," Leah said, and he groaned, the same way Jeremy used to, knowing that "we'll see" really meant no. For a moment guilt over losing his son stabbed deep.

Leah gave Noelle a quick hug and smiled at Caleb as they gathered their things together. But as soon as the door was closed behind their guests, Leah avoided Isaac's gaze and hustled Ben into their room to get ready for bed.

Isaac scrubbed his hands over his face, wishing she'd come back out so they could talk, but after five minutes stretched to ten and then to fifteen, he knew it wasn't happening.

His heart squeezed, but he tried to shake it off. He pulled out the disposable phone and called Hawk. To his utter surprise, his buddy answered.

"Yeah?"

There was so much to tell him that Isaac took a minute to formulate his thoughts. "Your partner, Trey Birchwood, was murdered by the same guy who tried to grab Leah and Ben. I managed to take a shell casing from the scene of the crime and plan to run it through the system. While I was out looking for Wade Sharkey, I stumbled across Stan's Liquor Store, which appears to be a common place to do gun-sale business. I recognized one of the guys as going to Saint Jermaine's, but I can't think of his name, other than he went by the nickname Steel. He recognized me, too, and tried to kill me."

"You've been busy," Hawk said, in a tone so quiet Isaac could barely hear him. Hawk had to be hiding somewhere, and Isaac wished his friend would trust him enough to tell him where. "I thought I told you to stay out of this. Your only job is to watch over Leah and Ben."

Isaac reined in his temper with an effort. "Look, knock it off, okay? You can't do this alone. Besides, you don't know your sister very well if you think she's content with sitting here doing nothing while you're out there fighting for your life. I'm going to text you this photo, and I need you to tell me this guy's name."

"Okay, I'll call you back."

He disconnected from the line and Isaac blew out a heavy breath as he sent the photo of the guy who'd shot at him to Hawk's phone. It didn't take long for his friend to call him back.

"His name is Joey Stainwhite, but everyone called him Steel because he had nerves of iron when it came to doing anything dangerous. And he's definitely in this with Wade."

"That's what I thought. Okay, where are you? I think we'd be better off working as a team."

"Not yet. I'm…in the middle of something."

Hawk's evasiveness was really starting to make Isaac mad. "Don't you care about your sister at all? Don't you understand how worried sick she is about you? What could be more important than coming in to work with us?"

Hawk didn't answer right away, and Isaac hoped that he'd knocked some sense into his buddy's thick skull. "Soon, I promise," he finally said.

"What about your ATF contact? Have you tried him?"

"I have, but no answer yet."

"Okay, I'll give you until morning, and then we're coming to get you whether you like it or not."

"I hear you. Gotta go." And just that quickly the connection between them was broken.

Isaac ground his teeth in frustration and just barely managed not to throw the disposable phone across the room. He spun around, intending to head to the kitchen table, but stopped abruptly when he saw Leah hovering just outside the doorway to her room. From the shocked expression on her face, she'd obviously heard his side of the call with her brother.

He mentally kicked himself for being so stupid, but how was he to know she'd come out? Unless she'd overheard him and had come to find out what was going on? No, he didn't think he'd been talking that loudly.

Well, at least not until the end of the conversation. He knew he'd lost his temper then.

Leah was watching him, her dark hair curling around her shoulders, her eyes clinging to his, and he had to swallow hard to stop himself from going over there to pull her into his arms.

Bad idea, he reminded himself. Really, really bad idea.

"I'm sorry for losing my temper like that," he said helplessly, thinking he hadn't apologized this much since his wife had filed for divorce and left, taking Jeremy when she'd moved in with her new boyfriend. The one she'd had an affair with while he'd been working so many extra hours.

The one who'd eventually killed her and Isaac's son.

"None of this is your fault, Isaac," Leah said softly. "You're in the middle of this mess because my brother dragged you into it."

She was mostly right, but he shook his head anyway. "This is what cops do, Leah. We fight the bad guys and try to put them behind bars. If I wasn't working on this case, I'd be working on something else."

A flash of pain darkened her eyes and he mentally kicked himself again, harder. Why in the world had he reminded her about his dangerous career?

"What did Shane say?" she asked, stepping closer.

Isaac curled his fingers into fists to keep from reaching for her. "He knew the name of the guy who shot at me, which is good news. Now I can put a warrant out for his arrest."

"I heard you trying to convince him to meet with us," she said, coming closer still. So close her cinnamon-and-spice scent teased his nostrils. "Thank you for doing that."

He shrugged, since his attempt had fallen on deaf ears. "I don't like him being out there alone."

"He's stubborn, isn't he?" Leah said with a wry smile. "Guess that's another trait he gets from our father."

Isaac lifted a brow. "A trait you share," he pointed out drily.

When she took another step toward him, he needed every ounce of willpower he had not to take a step back. Didn't she realize the effect she had on him?

Obviously not.

"Isaac…" Her voice trailed off as she reached out to touch his arm, the heat of her small hand burning through the fleece of his sweatshirt. "I'm so glad you weren't hurt," she whispered.

His thoughts scattered, but there was one thing he knew he needed to tell her. "I prayed and immediately felt calm. And I owe that to you."

A smile bloomed on her face and suddenly he couldn't help himself.

He pulled her into his arms and kissed her, ignoring the tiny voice in his head that warned he might be making a mistake.

Because having Leah in his arms felt exactly right.

NINE

After a momentary shock of surprise, Leah melted against Isaac, savoring his kiss. It had been so long since she'd kissed a man, she'd completely forgotten how wonderful it was to share this intimacy. To be held protectively, as if she was something precious.

To be wanted.

And cared for.

She couldn't say how long the kiss lasted, but when Isaac lifted his head to breathe, she clung to his broad shoulders for a long, heartbreaking moment. He was so tall, so different from her husband.

Wait a minute. What was she doing? She'd vowed not to love another man after Elliot died. She shouldn't be doing this. Kissing Isaac was not smart.

Regretfully, she pulled away and stepped back, drawing a deep, cleansing breath even though she knew she wouldn't forget the impact of Isaac's kiss.

Ever.

"Leah," he began, but she quickly shook her head.

"Don't," she begged. "Don't apologize or say anything else, either. Let's just enjoy the moment we shared and move on."

Isaac's eyebrows levered up and then pulled together into a frown as he stared at her for a long moment, his mouth drawn into a thin, tense line. His dark eyes were difficult to read, and she told herself she didn't want to know what he was thinking, because she was already hanging on to her control by a thin thread.

"Good night, Isaac," she said, forcing herself to turn and head into the bedroom she shared with Ben.

As she was closing the door behind her, she heard his husky voice. "Good night, Leah."

She needed every ounce of willpower flowing through her bloodstream to close the door. Even then, she leaned weakly against it. No matter how much she was attracted to Isaac, entering into a relationship with him or with any man wasn't what she wanted. She couldn't imagine losing another husband. Maybe Noelle found a way to deal with Caleb's dangerous job, but then again, Noelle likely hadn't lost her father to the perils of being a cop.

And certainly Noelle hadn't watched her mother drink herself to death as a result of that loss.

Feeling stronger in her resolve, Leah washed her face and brushed her teeth in the bathroom, then crawled into bed. But sleep wouldn't come. She stared blindly up at the ceiling, rehashing everything that had just happened. She'd been so happy to hear that Isaac had prayed when he was in danger. There wasn't a greater honor than helping people find their way to the Lord.

And what she needed now was the power of prayer to deal with her own rioting emotions.

She closed her eyes and cleared her mind, opening her heart and her soul to God.

As Your willing servant, I ask You to show me the way, Lord. Provide me the wisdom I need to guide Isaac and the strength to face whatever the future holds. And please, Lord, keep my son and my brother safe in Your care. Amen.

Isaac dropped onto the edge of the sofa and cradled his head in his hands. *Nice move, kissing her senseless. What in the world were you thinking?*

Yeah, that was the problem, all right. Thinking hadn't really entered into the equation at all. And he was mad at himself for getting emotionally involved with Leah in the first place, especially since she'd made her position on not dating cops loud and clear.

Marriage and cops didn't go well together. He'd learned that when Becky had left him. So why was he even entertaining the idea of trying again?

For a moment he considered what he might do if he gave up being a cop. But the instant the idea entered his mind, he shoved it aside.

No way was he giving up his entire career for a woman. Besides, being an officer was who he was. His team meant a lot to him. Being a part of something good, putting the bad guys behind bars, was important to him, as well.

Anyone who truly cared about him wouldn't ask him to give it up.

So why didn't that make him feel any better?

Maybe the problem was really his. He couldn't give enough to a relationship because he gave everything to his career. It wouldn't be fair to drag any woman into marriage. And especially not Leah.

From now on, he needed to keep his distance from her.

He stood and crossed over to the window, which overlooked the back parking lot. He'd tucked his car beneath a tree, hoping to make the bullet hole in the windshield less obvious. The mud over the license plate was still intact, and he'd made sure he hadn't been followed.

But then he remembered the canister of tear gas flying through the window of their first hotel room. That wouldn't happen here, since they were up on the second floor, but the fact that a dirty cop was involved bothered him.

Cops had way more resources available to them than the average layperson did.

He dropped the curtain and crossed over to the kitchen table, where the laptop was sitting. Hawk had given him the name Joey Stainwhite, so Isaac made the call to the department dispatcher to put a warrant out for Joey's arrest.

Once that task was completed, he tried to do a search on the guy, but of course he didn't find much. Other than the fact that Joey had a very similar police record as Wade.

Had they served time together? Isaac checked the records and wasn't surprised to find they had in fact done so. How had they gone from petty crime to dealing illegal weapons?

He stared at the computer screen, realizing that Wade and Joey had to be lower-level operatives. There had to be someone higher up who was the brains behind the operation.

And based on what Hawk had told him, the head honcho was very possibly a dirty cop.

A flashing red light coming through the crack in the curtains caught his eye. He scowled and leaped up to cross over to the window. When he looked outside, he could see a cop had someone pulled over.

Nothing to worry about—the officer likely was handing out a speeding ticket or DUI. But Isaac stayed by the window anyway, watching to make sure the policeman didn't stumble upon his car.

It seemed to take forever for the cop to finish, and even then he didn't leave right away. He had turned off the red flashing lights on the squad car, but what in the world was he doing out there?

Isaac was getting more and more nervous until finally the officer pulled away, making a wide U-turn before heading back out onto the highway.

For a moment Isaac debated waking Leah and Ben to head to a new hotel, chiding himself for not moving earlier.

No, he couldn't do it. There was no evidence of real danger, and after swimming all evening, Ben no doubt needed a good night's sleep.

But even though, logically, he knew they were safe, Isaac stretched out on the sofa rather than going into the bedroom. He planned to be ready, just in case.

Leah and Ben were his top priority. Anyone daring to come in would have to go through him to get to them.

Leah woke up the next morning to the sound of Ben's laughter coming from the living room. For a moment she was reminded of Saturday mornings when Elliot would get their son up so that she could sleep in.

The old, familiar pang of grief didn't follow on the heels of that thought, a fact that surprised her. There were times she had trouble remembering her husband's face, although she had pictures.

None with her now, though.

Leah had tried to keep Elliot's memory alive for Ben, but he'd been only a year old when his father died, far too young to retain any real memories.

And for some reason, that thought didn't make her sad this morning.

She leaped out of bed, more eager to see Isaac again than she should be. After hurrying through her shower and blow-drying her hair, she pulled on her jeans and sweater before following the enticing smell of breakfast.

"Good morning." Isaac greeted her cheerfully, despite looking rumpled and exhausted.

"Good morning," she responded lightly, unwilling to broach the subject of his sleepless night. After all, it had taken her far longer than it should have to fall asleep, thanks to his toe-curling kiss.

"Breakfast just arrived, so help yourself." Isaac gestured to the food waiting on the table. "And I found another place for us to stay tonight, one I'd like to run past you."

She frowned and took a seat at the kitchen table. "Another place? Why can't we stay here?"

Isaac shrugged and glanced at Ben. "I'll explain later. First, let's eat."

Leah waited for Isaac to sit down and was surprised when he folded his hands together, looking at her expectantly. She drew in a deep breath and bowed her head. "Dear Lord, we thank You for this wonderful food You've provided for us. We also thank You for keeping all of us safe from harm. We ask for Your grace and mercy as we begin our day. Amen."

"Amen," both Isaac and Ben echoed.

The food was delicious. She glanced around the suite, wishing they didn't have to leave. Had something happened last night? Something that had caused Isaac a restless night?

Ridiculous to assume he'd been kept awake by their kiss.

She really needed to get a grip already. They were dependent on each other for now, but as soon as Shane met up with them, they wouldn't need Isaac's help anymore. They'd go their separate ways.

She stared at her scrambled eggs, refusing to be depressed by the thought of Isaac leaving. Based on the hero worship in her son's eyes, she wasn't the only one who would miss him.

Her stomach twisted painfully and her previously ravenous appetite evaporated away. She pushed her food around for a few minutes before giving up the pretense.

"That was delicious. Thank you," she said, sliding away her half-eaten breakfast.

"You're welcome," Isaac said, frowning when he saw the amount of food she hadn't eaten. Thankfully, he didn't say anything more as she busied herself with cleaning up.

As soon as Ben and he were finished eating, she turned toward Isaac. "Today is Sunday, right? I'd really like to attend church services."

He looked surprised at her request, but then slowly nodded. "All right, we can go back to that church from the other night if you'd like."

"Great—thanks." That was one issue solved. "I also need to call in to work. I had the weekend off but I'm scheduled to work tomorrow morning. I need to give them time to find my replacement."

"Uh, sure. No problem. I've already taken a few personal days myself, but you might want to take the whole week off, since we have no idea when this will be over."

"I can't call in sick for a whole week," she said, horrified that he'd even suggest such a thing.

"I understand, but I don't want anyone at work to know where you are or what's going on. We wouldn't want to inadvertently put anyone at the hospital in danger."

She nodded and took the disposable phone into

the bedroom to make the call. What could she say that wouldn't be an outright lie? With a grimace she told the charge nurse on duty that she had some personal problems and couldn't come in to work. And when the woman tried to pry more information out of her, Leah quickly disconnected the call.

Good thing they were attending church, because she desperately needed the spiritual support right now.

She gathered their clothing and personal items together, packing everything into the duffel bag they'd purchased yesterday, which seemed like weeks ago. Then she hauled the duffel out to the living area.

"Here, I'd like to show you what I found," Isaac said, motioning her over. She dropped the bag on the floor near the door and crossed to the computer. "Check this place out. They have small two-bedroom cabins for rent, fairly cheap, since it's the off-season. And there's a playground for Ben, which I thought would be nice."

"Looks good," she agreed. "But it's pretty far away, isn't it?"

Isaac nodded. "Yeah, but I can't help thinking that being farther outside of town is better for us."

"What happened last night?" she asked.

"Nothing really, just a cop hanging out after he pulled someone over. Made me nervous, that's all." Isaac shut down the computer. "Are you ready to go?"

She nodded, and it didn't take long to check out of the hotel. What was surprising was that the bullet hole in the windshield was already repaired. "How did you get that done so fast?"

"Caleb made the call for first thing this morning. There's a company that drives out to where your car is located to fix broken or cracked windshields."

"Amazing," she muttered as Isaac stored their things in the trunk.

The ride to the church didn't take long, and just seeing the brick building with its stained-glass windows and steeple gave Leah a sense of coming home.

She wasn't sure what Isaac thought about attending church, since this wasn't a wedding or a funeral, but she was touched that he'd agreed regardless. With Ben sitting between them, she couldn't shake the idea that everyone around them likely thought they were a family.

She tried to concentrate on the service and the pastor's theme of forgiveness, but it wasn't easy. She kept glancing over at Isaac, amazed that he seemed to be intently following the sermon.

Did he need to forgive someone for something? And if so, why did she care?

It had taken time for her to fully forgive the

drunk driver who'd hit Elliot head-on in a crash that cost her husband his life. Since it was the man's third DUI offense, he'd gotten sentenced to seven years in prison for vehicular homicide. She prayed he'd see the error of his ways and would turn his life around once he was released from jail.

She silently prayed for Isaac to find peace in forgiveness. And when he took her hand in his during the Lord's Prayer, she couldn't prevent the tiny thrill of awareness that shimmered through her.

The service was over much too quickly, but she was glad for the opportunity to attend. They made their way outside into the bright sunlight. The spring temperatures were finally warming up, and she couldn't help smiling when Ben let out a whoop and ran up and down the rows of cars.

"Over here, Ben," Isaac called, gesturing at their vehicle.

Her son had a lot of pent-up energy, because he continued running around with his arms spread wide, pretending to be an airplane.

Isaac took off after him, and she stood by the car, watching the two of them together. Isaac didn't yell at the boy, but lifted him up and flew him around and around like a plane.

"Do it again, Mr. Isaac, do it again," he begged.

"Once more and then we have to leave, all

right?" Isaac waited until he nodded before swinging him in a circle again.

Ben was giggling madly as they finally returned to the car. Leah wanted to thank Isaac for being so kind to her son, but her throat felt too tight and she found herself blinking back the sting of tears.

"All set?" Isaac asked, glancing over at her.

"Yes," she managed to answer, avoiding his gaze by buckling her seat belt.

The drive along the country highway was nice and quiet on a Sunday afternoon. Isaac seemed to know where he was going, so she tried to sit back and enjoy the fact that they weren't running for their lives for once.

"We're almost there," Isaac said before Ben could ask for the fifth time. "The road leading to the log-cabin rentals is just up ahead."

The area around the cabins looked sparsely populated, and Leah couldn't help wondering if that was part of the reason Isaac had chosen the place. She smiled when Ben let out a whoop as he caught sight of the playground.

"Can I go play, Mom? Can I?" he asked anxiously.

She glanced over at Isaac and nodded. "Yes, but you have to wait until we get checked in, okay?"

Her son didn't appreciate the wait, but soon Isaac returned with the keys to their cabin. He handed one to her. "We're in number seven. I'll haul our stuff inside if you want to take Ben to the playground."

"Sure, that would be great." She slid out of the passenger seat and then opened the back door to help Ben out. He'd already unlatched the booster-seat strap by himself.

He ran ahead, teeming with exuberance. She followed more slowly, enjoying watching him. She was so fortunate to have him as a part of her life.

Despite the sun, the wind still held a chill, so after about forty-five minutes, she called him over. "It's time to go in."

"Okay." Her son had her dark hair and fair skin, and his cheeks were rosy from the cold. They walked down the path, finding cabin seven without difficulty.

Isaac was on the phone when they arrived, so she tried to keep Ben quiet so they wouldn't disturb him. She took off Ben's coat and glanced around their latest home away from home. The cabin was a tad smaller than the suite had been, but the two bedrooms flanking the living area were almost the same. Leah hung up their coats on a wooden rack behind the door and went to stand next to the blaze that Isaac had going in the fireplace.

He was scribbling notes on the stationery he

must have taken from their previous hotel. "What else?" he asked when he'd finished.

There was another long pause as he listened to whoever was talking on the other end of the line, probably Caleb or Declan.

"Okay, call me as soon as you find something else," he said before disconnecting from the call.

"What's going on?" she asked.

Isaac glanced at Ben and then shrugged. "New details from the crime-scene techs."

She appreciated that he didn't want to say too much in front of her son, but she had a stake in this investigation, too. "Ben, why don't you get your cars out so you can play for a while?"

"Okay," he agreed.

"The room closest to the fireplace is yours," Isaac said when Ben headed in the wrong direction. "Be careful—it's hot."

Leah waited until her son was well out of earshot. "Tell me what they found."

"The shell casing is the same type found at the scene of an unsolved murder," he admitted. "Young man by the name of Enrique Morales."

She stared at Isaac blankly, thinking there had to be more to the story than this. "So, what does that mean?"

"Enrique also spent time at Saint Jermaine's school for delinquent teens," Isaac admitted. "And he was murdered exactly one week ago today."

She shivered, not liking the strong link to the place. "You think he was part of this whole illegal gun scheme?"

"Can't say for sure, but I do think it's possible. And if that is the case, then I can't help but wonder how many more people will die before we figure out who the top guy is," Isaac said grimly.

Leah swallowed hard, thinking about Shane. It was creepy the way everything seemed to revolve around Saint Jermaine's, a place where both Isaac and Shane had been sentenced to over twelve years ago. It wasn't as if they'd spent years there, either; the time frame was better measured in months. But clearly, whatever criminal activity had started back then had resurrected in the here and now.

Two deaths associated with this mess so far: Trey Birchwood and now Enrique Morales.

She had to convince her brother to meet with Isaac and her soon. Before he became the next victim.

TEN

Isaac pushed away from the table feeling restless. The puzzle pieces were beginning to fall into place, but there were still way too many missing holes. And worse, he wasn't sure what steps he could take next to fill in the blanks.

"I want to talk to Shane," Leah said abruptly. "He has to let us come and pick him up."

Isaac nodded, agreeing with her concern. "I told him the same thing last night. So far he hasn't been willing to accept our help." He didn't add that the main reason Hawk was keeping his distance was because he didn't want to put Leah and Ben in any danger.

Hawk would rather die in the line of duty than risk the innocent lives of the people he loved.

And frankly, Isaac couldn't blame him. He'd do the same thing if the situation was reversed.

"Give me his number," Leah insisted. "Maybe I can convince him."

Isaac hesitated, but reached for his phone. Why

not have Leah talk to him? Maybe hearing from his sister would help change Hawk's mind about coming in. "Here, use mine—he might not recognize your number." He watched Leah make the call, thinking he'd been more than ready to pick up Hawk last night. In fact, he'd pushed him as hard as he could, but to no avail.

Of course, Hawk didn't answer. Isaac knew by the brevity of the call that his buddy must have his phone off.

Leah let out a heavy sigh of frustration. "He's ignoring us," she muttered.

"Or he's in a place where he can't talk," Isaac pointed out.

"So now what?" she asked, throwing up her hands. "We can't just sit here and wait. We need to do something."

He didn't want to remind her about what had happened the last time he'd tried to *do* something. The bullet hole in his windshield had been repaired, but the seat cushion where he'd dug out the bullet was still a mess.

"Here, program the number into your phone, so that you have it, just in case."

She did as he suggested. "I still don't like the fact that there is nothing we can do to help him."

"I know," Isaac admitted. "Listen, why don't you and Ben enjoy some downtime?"

Leah rolled her eyes but didn't say anything

more. He understood she was chafing at being holed up in a small log cabin as much as he was. But he didn't have another option for her.

Belatedly, he remembered the gun they'd recovered from the mall shooting incident. So much had happened that he hadn't had time to ask someone to check for the weapon in the evidence room. "There might be one thing I can do," he said slowly. He called Declan's number, but his friend didn't answer. The thought of calling Caleb after his buddy had gone above and beyond to help him out last evening didn't sit well with him, either. Isaac didn't want to keep dragging his buddies away from their families.

The newest member of their team, Jenna Reed, had been with him during that mall incident. Maybe she'd be willing to check out the evidence room and see if there had been any headway on the ballistics evidence, as well.

Despite being blonde and petite, Jenna had surprised them all with her incredible sharpshooting skills. She might have placed second behind Caleb, but not by much. Yes, she had a bit of a chip on her shoulder, always determined to carry her own weight, sometimes to the point of being ridiculous. But she tolerated the general ribbing from the rest of the guys without getting too bent out of shape.

He called the dispatch center for her number,

and once he phoned her, she surprised him by picking up on the second ring. "Reed," she said curtly.

"Hey, Jenna, it's Isaac. I need a favor if you have a few minutes."

"Sure. What's up?" There was a hint of surprise in her tone, as if she hadn't expected him to call her for help.

He quickly explained what he wanted and she readily agreed. "I'll check out the evidence room and search on the ballistics report. Is this the number you want me to use to call you back when I have something?"

"Yeah. And, Jenna? Thanks."

"No problem."

He disconnected, once again thinking how great it was to have a team of people he trusted. Too bad Hawk didn't have the same level of teamwork within his district.

"Jenna?" Leah echoed. "Is she one of the dispatchers?"

Was Leah jealous of Jenna? No, had to be his imagination. "She's a sharpshooter for the SWAT team."

A tiny frown puckered Leah's brow. "And you trust her? The same way you trust Caleb and Declan?"

"Caleb and Declan are my best friends, so no, I don't trust Jenna in the exact same way. But she's a good cop and I've been in a few tactical situations with her. She can hold her own."

Leah flashed a lopsided smile. "Sorry to be on edge. I just don't want to risk anything happening to my brother. I know I'm driving you crazy, but I just can't imagine what Shane must be going through."

"I care about your brother, too, Leah," he reminded her. "I don't want to see anything happen to him, either."

She nodded, her expression thoughtful. "He and I have always been close, but even more so in the past few years since our parents died. Shane helped support me through nursing school, after Mom passed away. I'm not sure if I would have finished without him."

Isaac nodded. "He's super proud of everything you've accomplished."

"Goes both ways," she assured him. "I'm proud of him and you, too. Especially after the way you and Shane both turned your life around after being at Saint Jermaine's. I wonder why Wade didn't make the same decision?"

"I think Wade's lawyer must have pulled some strings to get him sentenced to the school rather than sent to jail," Isaac said with a frown. "He had several run-ins with the law prior to the time he was sentenced to Saint Jermaine's. The rest of us didn't. As first-time offenders, we were given the opportunity for a second chance."

"I know that Shane's public defender made a big deal out of the way we lost our father," Leah said softly. "I think he used it as a way to garner sympathy for the self-destructive choices that Shane made."

Isaac nodded, knowing his own attorney had done something similar. Not that he was anxious to share the details of his personal life with Leah. She and Shane had suffered a blow when their father died, but at least they'd had a dad. He'd tried to find his dad when he was eighteen, but his father had refused to see or talk to him. Isaac had moved on, but always wondered why his dad refused to have anything to do with him.

"What about you?" Leah asked, leaning forward and pinning him with her clear blue eyes. "How was it that your lawyer managed to convince a judge to let you go to the school?"

He hesitated, wondering just how much he should tell her. "My mom… Well, let's just say she had problems. There were a lot of different men in her life, none of which seemed to hang around very long. She worked in a hair and nail salon, but we were constantly struggling to make ends meet." He shrugged and averted his gaze, not wanting to see the sympathy reflected in Leah's. "I was arrested for selling drugs because we didn't have any food at home. I think my story and the fact that it was a first drug-possession offense helped him plead my case."

"You had it rough, didn't you?" Leah asked softly.

He waved it off. "I'm nothing special. Lots of kids have it rough." He walked over to the fire and put another log on, wishing Leah would change the subject.

"Mommy, come look!" Ben said in an excited whisper.

Isaac followed Leah into the bedroom, hanging in the doorway as she and Ben stared through the window. Ben pointed at a spot in the glass. "Deers," he whispered in awe.

Sure enough, two white-tailed deer, likely a mother and her baby, were standing about fifty yards away, peeling bark off one of the trees. If they were aware of the humans watching from the window, they didn't show it.

"They're beautiful, aren't they?" Leah whispered, putting her arm around Ben's shoulders.

"We have to talk quiet so we don't scare them, right?" he asked.

"That's right," she agreed.

Isaac moved back to the living room, feeling a pang in his chest. Leah was a great mother to Ben, and watching them together reminded him of how much he'd missed with Becky and Jeremy.

His fault for not cutting back on his overtime hours. His fault for letting his career mean more to him than his family.

His fault for not loving Becky enough.

He dropped onto the edge of the sofa and ran his hand over his hair. He and Becky had gotten married too young and had Jeremy just a year later, but he hadn't loved her the way Caleb and Deck loved their wives. He could admit now what a mess he'd made of his life.

Leah was right to stay far away from him. He was a cop and a guy who didn't know how to find the right balance between his career and his personal life.

It was easier to focus on the former and ignore the latter.

When his disposable cell phone rang, he reached for it gratefully. He recognized Jenna's number. "Hey, Jenna, did you find something?"

"Yes, and I think you've been holding out on me," she accused without heat. "The ballistics from the gun we recovered at the mall shooting is the same type and caliber found in two recent murders."

Two murders? He gripped the phone tightly. "Enrique Morales was one of them, right?"

"Bingo. And the second is a dead cop by the name of Trey Birchwood," Jenna said.

Isaac's gut tightened at the news, even though this was exactly what he'd suspected.

"Birchwood and Morales weren't murdered with the exact same weapon as the one used in the mall shooting, but it's the same make, model and caliber of bullet. So tell me, how did you know?" Jenna demanded.

"Educated guess," he hedged.

"Don't give me that line," she snapped. "If you don't want to tell, fine, but don't pretend you're not in the middle of some sort of investigation. And you know I need to let Griff Vaughn know what you've found, since it's connected to the mall shooting."

"Look, Jenna, I'm helping out a friend who just happens to be working undercover, okay?" Isaac couldn't stop her from going to their boss, but he wanted to make sure she understood the gravity of the situation. "Things are happening pretty fast, and hopefully, I'll know more by tomorrow. If you really feel the need to tell Griff what you know, that's fine. But trust me, I'm working on it and hope to know more soon."

There was a long pause on the other end as Jenna considered his words. "Okay, fine. I'll hold off for now. But if you need help, call me. We're supposed to be part of a team, remember?"

He couldn't help but grin at her annoyed

tone. "Yeah, I remember. And I will call you if I need help."

She snorted. "Yeah, right. Later, Morrison." She clicked off before he could say anything more.

Isaac realized that Jenna was all too aware of how close he was to Declan and Caleb, and why shouldn't he be? They were his best friends. But maybe Jenna felt left out by their closeness.

Nothing he could do about that now, but he made a mental note to mention the issue to his pals once this was over.

Right now, he had bigger concerns to think about. Wade and his cohorts in crime were part of an underground ring selling illegal guns to criminals. And now three crime scenes were linked to the same type of gun.

Were there other crimes, too? He had to assume so, since he knew Wade had to be doing this for a while.

But if they put out an arrest warrant on Wade Sharkey right now, the top guy might get away. What if he left town, only to set up shop somewhere else, in another city or state?

No, they needed to figure out who was the mastermind of the gunrunning ring and take him down as soon as possible.

While keeping Leah and Ben safe at the same time.

A monumental task, at best.

* * *

Leah encouraged Ben to play a card game with her in an effort to keep him entertained. After several rounds of Go Fish, he lost interest and decided he wanted to play his video game. Left alone, she pulled out the Bible she'd found in a drawer and turned to her favorite Psalm, 23:4.

"Even though I walk through the darkest valley, I will fear no evil. For You are with me; Your rod and Your staff, they comfort me."

The words soothed her soul and helped to keep her calm. She could hear Isaac in the other room, tapping on the laptop, and even though she continued to read the rest of the psalm, she found herself wondering what Isaac was working on.

After a few minutes, she gave up and set the Bible aside. Ben was still focused on his game, so she crossed into the living room to look over Isaac's shoulder.

His expression was intense as he remained focused on the screen, and for a moment she admired his square jaw, his sandy-brown hair and deep brown eyes. She caught a whiff of shaving cream and noticed that he'd nicked himself earlier that morning along the lower edge of his jaw. For a moment she was tempted to place a tiny kiss there.

Idiot, she chided herself. She cleared her throat

and forced herself to take a step back. "Find anything new?"

"Not yet," he muttered. He pushed away from the computer and glanced up at her. "Are you hungry? We can think about what you and Ben would like for dinner."

"I'm okay for now, although didn't we pass a diner on the way in? Might be nice to have something different."

"We can get something to eat at the diner, no problem," Isaac agreed.

She noticed he'd made a list of notes as he worked on the computer. "What is all this?" she asked, running her index finger down the page. "A list of crimes in the Milwaukee area?"

"Yes, as a matter of fact, they are." Isaac didn't say anything more, so she sat down and began reading through the list.

It took a minute for her to see the pattern. "These are all crimes involving guns. You think these are all linked to the illegal sales?"

Isaac glanced at her and nodded. "Yes. I didn't realize that armed robberies and other gun-related crimes have doubled in the past three months." He rubbed the back of his neck and then tapped the computer screen. "I found an article from a few weeks ago, describing a recent press conference by the chief of police regarding the city's plan to create a task force to address the spike in crime."

Realization dawned. "Shane was sent under-cover as part of the task force."

"You got it. Plus it's an election year for the mayor, so I'm sure he's not thrilled about having these stats released mere weeks before the good citizens get to vote on whether or not he gets to keep his job."

"Okay, I can see why this is important, but we already knew Shane was working undercover. How does any of this help us find him?"

"I don't know. I'm just trying to get a sense of the bigger picture here," Isaac admitted. "Every little bit helps."

"I think it's tedious," she muttered with a sigh.

Surprisingly, Isaac grinned. "That's because you think cops spend all their time shooting bad guys. There are a lot of tedious aspects to the job. And you're used to constant action, working on trauma patients that come rolling through the E.R."

"True." Ironic how much she missed her job now that she was forced to call off work for a few days. All the hustle and bustle of taking care of sick patients, never knowing what was coming through the doors next, made it a job that was never, ever boring.

Similar to Isaac's job in many ways, without the inherent danger, of course.

She purposefully shied away from thinking

about Isaac being in danger. Although at the same time, watching him perform the investigational aspect of his job was oddly reassuring.

Why couldn't she seem to get Isaac out of her mind? She'd been blessed to have found love with her husband. There was no reason to go down that path again. She believed what her pastor told her as far as Elliot being in a much better place, but that didn't mean she didn't miss him. That Ben didn't miss having a father.

Some people went their whole life without finding someone to love. She should be glad for the short time she'd had with Elliot, even if their marriage hadn't been perfect. What marriage was?

She didn't need to find someone else to take his place.

Isaac's musky scent was messing with her ability to concentrate, so she stood and crossed over to the fireplace. The glowing logs were still radiating heat, making the cabin warm and cozy.

When the sound of a cell phone broke the silence, she glanced over at Isaac, figuring it was Jenna or one of the other SWAT members calling him.

"It's your brother," Isaac said. "Do you want to talk to him?"

"Absolutely." She took the phone and tried to calm her racing heart. "Hello?" she said breathlessly. "Shane, is that you?"

"Yes, it's me." Her brother's familiar voice sent a wave of relief washing over her. Even if he was speaking so quietly she could barely hear him. "Why are you answering Ice's phone?"

"Because I wanted to talk to you. Are you okay?" she asked. "I've been so worried."

"You're not alone, are you?" Shane asked abruptly. "Ice is still there with you, right?"

She glanced over her shoulder at Isaac, who was watching her and listening intently. "Yes, he's here, keeping me and Ben safe. But I want to see you, Shane. Tell us where you are and we'll come and get you."

"Not yet," her brother hedged. "I'm getting close to finding some answers."

Her patience with his constant evasiveness was wearing thin. Leah was just about to give him a piece of her mind when she heard a loud noise, followed by her brother letting out a strangled cry of pain.

She tightened her grip on the phone. "Shane? What happened? Are you okay?"

But he didn't answer. There was nothing but an eerie silence on the other end of the line.

Her fingers shook with fear as she quickly called him back. But still no answer.

Tears blurred her vision and a sob rose in her throat. Her brother was hurt or worse, but she didn't even know how to find him.

What if he died before help arrived?

She couldn't bear the thought of losing her brother. Shane was her rock of support, as well as being a father figure for her son.

Please, Lord, keep Shane safe in Your care!

ELEVEN

Isaac watched the blood drain out of Leah's face and knew right away that something was wrong. He stood and crossed over to her, reaching for her hand. "What happened?"

The dazed expression in her blue eyes wrenched his heart. "There was a loud noise and Shane cried out as if he was hurt, and then he disconnected from the call." She shook her head helplessly. "We have to find him, Isaac. We have to find him!"

He wished it were that easy. Hawk hadn't been very forthright about any aspect of this case, which left Isaac stumbling around in the dark. He wanted to knock some sense into her brother, but right now, Leah was his bigger concern.

Her devastation was impossible to ignore, and she needed support. He slipped his phone into his pocket and then pulled her close, wrapping his arms around her in a reassuring hug.

For a moment Leah held herself stiff, but then

with a strangled sob she burrowed against him, clinging to him as if she wouldn't ever let go.

Isaac let her cry, wishing he could think of something reassuring to say.

But words failed him. Because he knew Hawk was in big trouble. For all they knew, his buddy could be dead.

As much as he wanted to protect Leah from the truth, she knew full well what her brother faced. Isaac kissed the top of her head, wishing there was more he could do for her.

Leah didn't cry for long. After a few minutes she sniffled loudly and lifted her head so that she could look up at him. "Isaac, will you pray with me?"

He gazed down into her watery blue eyes, knowing he could not refuse her request. "Of course I will."

Her tremulous smile made any embarrassment he might have felt inconsequential. He led her over to the sofa and sat down at an angle so he could partially face her.

Leah sat beside him and clasped both his hands in hers. She bowed her head and he followed her lead, bowing his, as well.

She was silent for a moment, so he took a deep breath and began to speak, hoping he would know the correct words to say. "Dear Lord, we ask You to watch over Shane, keeping him safe in Your care."

"And we ask that You guide him home to us," Leah added.

How was it that he hadn't realized how easy it was to pray? Isaac continued, "Lord, we also ask that You keep the three of us safe in Your care."

"And we ask that You guide us on Your chosen path. Amen."

"Amen," he echoed. He couldn't deny the sense of peace that washed over him and realized, not for the first time, just how powerful leaning on God's strength could be. And how important it was to have faith to guide you through the difficult times.

"Thank you, Isaac," Leah murmured, still holding on to his hands. "I'm thrilled that you believe in God and have begun to trust in His goodness and strength."

He surprised himself by wanting to share more with her. "You know, both Caleb and Declan have discovered faith in the past year, and I resisted following in their footsteps," he admitted. "Now I can't figure out why I did that. Why didn't I trust my closest friends enough to believe?"

Leah tilted her head to the side, an ebony curl brushing against her cheek. His fingers itched to smooth it away. "Giving up your old beliefs can be scary," she said. "But once you let go and open your heart to God, you realize that believing in Him isn't hard or scary at all."

"You're right—it's not one bit difficult." Isaac stared at their joined hands for a long moment. The choices he'd made in the past still haunted him. Mistakes that had cost him his wife and son.

"What's wrong, Isaac?" Leah asked. "You look troubled."

For the first time since losing his son, he found himself wanting to talk about what had happened. "I wish I would have found God sooner," he admitted. "I can't help thinking that if I had, my son might still be alive today."

"I didn't realize you had a son," Leah murmured, her eyes full of sadness. "Tell me about him."

"Jeremy was a great kid. He was always happy. He loved dump trucks and front-end loaders— he spent hours in the sandbox pretending to be a construction worker." The memory didn't bring the same level of sorrow that it had in the past.

"He sounds amazing," Leah said.

"He was." Isaac felt his chest tighten as he forced out the rest. "And it's my fault he's dead."

"I don't believe that," she scoffed gently. "You would never hurt your son."

The band around Isaac's chest was so tight it hurt to breathe. "You're right—I wouldn't hurt him intentionally, but my actions caused my wife to leave me, taking our three-year-old with her. Geoff, her new boyfriend, was charming when he wanted to be, but had a nasty temper when crossed."

Leah shifted on the sofa, putting her arm around Isaac's shoulders. "What did he do?"

He tensed for a moment. He hadn't told anyone the details of what had happened that night. The news had sensationalized the story to the point that he'd always avoided talking about it. "Becky had an affair with him, because I worked too many hours, putting my career before my family. She filed for divorce, left me and took Jeremy with her. I fought for joint custody and won. I went over to pick up my son at their house…" For a moment he couldn't continue.

Leah didn't say anything. She simply hugged him and waited for him to gather himself together.

"I heard shouting as I pulled up. I hurried up to the house and banged on the front door, demanding to be let in. I heard a gunshot and went crazy. I kicked open the door and saw Geoff holding a gun to Jeremy's head. I begged him not to shoot, but he killed my son and then turned the gun on himself."

"Oh, Isaac, I can't imagine how horrible that must have been for you," Leah murmured. "I'm so sorry you had to go through that."

"I probably could have saved him from shooting himself," he continued, wanting Leah to hear everything. "But I didn't move. Didn't do anything to stop him from taking his own life. I learned later from Becky's friend that she was going to leave him and come back to me. That's why Geoff killed her, killed my son and then himself. And I should have stopped him. I should have made him go to prison for what he did."

"You were in shock from losing your wife and son. I can't imagine anything more terrible. But that man's choices are not your fault," Leah said. "He chose to hurt your ex-wife and your son. He chose to take his own life. You're not responsible for his actions."

"Maybe not," Isaac agreed. He forced himself to meet Leah's gaze. "But I'm responsible for my actions, and I neglected my family. Neglected my marriage and my son. If I hadn't, Becky wouldn't have left me in the first place." He swallowed hard and forced himself to meet Leah's gaze. "And that is a choice I have to live with for the rest of my life."

Leah rested her head on Isaac's shoulder, inwardly reeling from what he'd been through. The very idea of losing Ben the way he'd lost his son, Jeremy, made her feel sick to her stomach. How terrible to have your child's life taken by someone else. She couldn't even imagine the terror Isaac had lived with.

But she needed to help him understand that God forgave all sins. Isaac wouldn't ever be able to move on if he didn't learn how to forgive Geoff and Becky.

And himself.

"I know a little about what you're going through," she said in a low tone. "Losing my husband when he was killed by a drunk driver—and Ben was barely a year old—was a terrible ordeal. I wouldn't have gotten through any of those days after the funeral if it wasn't for my faith. I went to church daily, leaned on our pastor for support. Even with my faith and the help of Shane and our pastor, there were many dark days."

Isaac turned and pulled her more fully into his arms. His masculine scent was soothing and she inhaled deeply, wishing she could stay here like this with him forever. "I'm sorry you had to go through that," he murmured. "I know your brother made sure that guy who hit him went to jail for a long time."

"Yes, he did. But there's more to the story," she admitted. "Something that I didn't even tell my brother about."

"What happened?" Isaac asked in a curt tone. "Did Elliot hurt you?"

"Not physically," she hastened to assure him.

"But I learned later he wasn't coming home from work, the way everyone thought. He was coming from his colleague's condo. His female colleague's condo."

There was a heavy moment of silence. "I'm sure your husband had a good reason to be there," Isaac said slowly. "Don't automatically think the worst."

She pressed her lips together and shook her head. "Not according to the colleague. Victoria claimed they were in love and that Elliot was making plans to leave me."

"I don't believe it," Isaac protested hotly. "You can't trust her story. For all you know, she made the whole thing up as a way to hurt you."

He wasn't telling her anything she hadn't told herself. "Maybe," Leah allowed. "I've gone over every conversation Elliot and I had over the months prior to his death. He never gave me any indication that he wasn't happy. Never so much as hinted at being bored or feeling tied down. But he also seemed distracted—I assumed, by his work. I've tried to tell myself to ignore what Victoria said, but there's always been just the tiniest sliver of a doubt lingering in the back of my mind. He did spend a lot of hours working. Working with her."

"Where is Victoria now?" Isaac demanded. "I

think I should pay her a visit. I'm sure I could get her to admit she made up the entire story."

Despite the seriousness of their conversation, a laugh bubbled up through Leah's throat at the thought of Isaac storming Victoria's condo and demanding the truth, her knight in shining armor. "Don't be ridiculous. Besides, she moved to a larger law firm in Chicago. I guess Milwaukee just wasn't big-time enough for her."

Isaac eased back, pinning Leah with his serious dark brown eyes. She had the crazy thought that she'd never get tired of looking up at him. "Don't give that woman the power to make you doubt your husband's love for a moment. Anyone who would say something like that to a grieving widow is meaner and lower than a snake. I have a feeling she lashed out at you because Elliot rebuffed her advances."

Leah couldn't help but smile. "Thank you, Isaac. I know you're probably right, and I shouldn't keep thinking about it. Espccially since I need to forgive and forget in order to move on. Something you should try to do, too," she added. "One thing I've learned is that life is too short to hold grudges. God has forgiven us for our sins and we need to do the same—forgive those who've sinned against us."

Isaac grimaced a little but nodded. "I understand what you're saying, and I promise to try. It's not going to be easy, but I'll try."

"That's all we can ask of ourselves," she agreed.

"Mommy, I'm starving," Ben said, running out from the bedroom where he'd been playing his video game.

"I'm hungry, too," she said, subtly pulling away from Isaac's embrace, hoping her son hadn't noticed just how close they had been. "Isaac, didn't you mention going to a diner?"

"Yes, I did. Come on—let's go." He reached out and squeezed her hand as she rose to her feet.

As they made their way out to the car, she realized that Isaac had lost his son as a result of someone else's actions, similar to the way she'd lost Elliot.

And neither one of those losses had anything to do with having a dangerous career.

Still, she couldn't seem to shake the idea that being in a relationship with Isaac would only cause more heartache. For her and possibly for Ben. What if things didn't work out? Her son would be crushed.

No, best thing for her would be to keep her distance from Isaac.

No matter how much she longed to stay in his arms, surrounded by his masculine scent and his strength.

* * *

Isaac couldn't deny feeling oddly content as he drove to the diner, a mile from their cabin, with Leah and Ben. This time, he led the before-meal prayer without feeling too self-conscious. "Dear Lord, thank You for providing this food we are about to eat and for watching over us as we seek the truth. We ask for You to forgive our sins and to guide us on Your chosen path. Amen."

"Amen," Leah and Ben echoed.

Leah's smile warmed Isaac's heart and he knew he was in danger of getting too emotionally involved, but couldn't seem to find the strength of will to pull back. Not after everything he and Leah had just shared.

She knew the worst about him, yet she hadn't pulled away in disgust. Hadn't condemned him for being a terrible husband and father. She'd accepted him despite his faults and had also confided in him. He was honored that she'd chosen to share her secrets.

After they'd placed their order, Ben announced he wanted to draw a picture, using the crayons and paper the family-friendly diner provided.

"What are you going to draw?" Leah asked, sipping her water.

"A picture for Mr. Isaac," Ben said, without looking up.

A lump formed in his throat, but he nodded and forced himself to respond. "That would be great, Ben."

It struck him at that moment just how much Hawk's death would affect the little boy. Isaac knew from what Leah had said that Ben looked up to his uncle, seeing him as a surrogate father. He'd been too young to have any real memories of his dad.

"Hmm... What's that?" Leah asked, pointing to something indistinguishable on the paper.

"That's Mr. Isaac's gun," Ben answered enthusiastically. "He saved you from the bad man, remember?"

For a moment fear darkened Leah's eyes, but then she smiled and nodded. "Of course I remember," she said, running her hand down her son's back. "We're very lucky to have Mr. Isaac protecting us, aren't we?"

Ben nodded, but continued to concentrate on his picture. The stick figure holding a gun might not be a strong resemblance to him, but it was close enough to make Isaac smile.

And to harden his resolve. He needed to find Hawk and soon. His buddy hadn't wanted him to contact his ATF agent, Cameron Walker, but with Hawk potentially injured or worse, Isaac didn't really have much of a choice.

"Excuse me for a minute," he said, tossing his

napkin aside and sliding out of the booth. Leah looked surprised, but no doubt assumed he needed to use the restroom.

Instead, he ducked outside and pulled out his disposable cell phone. There was no easy way to call directly to the Bureau of Alcohol, Tobacco and Firearms, but he knew that Nate Freemont, their SWAT technical guru, had connections.

He dialed Nate's number and waited impatiently for his teammate to answer. "Yeah?" Nate's tone was less than welcoming.

It took a minute for him to remember that Nate didn't recognize his number. "Hey, Nate, it's me, Isaac Morrison. Sorry about the unknown number, but I'm trying to stay off the grid."

"Hey, Isaac, what's up? Why the need to stay anonymous?"

The suspicion in Nate's tone wasn't reassuring. "I'm keeping a woman and her son safe as a favor for a friend of mine," he admitted, figuring that Nate would need something in order to help him out. "My friend is working undercover and needs help."

"What do you need from me?" Nate asked, the suspicion fading from his voice.

"Do you know anyone inside the ATF?" he asked. "I need to get in touch with an agent by the name of Cameron Walker."

"Yeah, I have connections there," Nate admitted. "It's Sunday evening, but let me see what I can do. Is this the number I should use to call you back?"

"Yeah, this number is good. Thanks, Nate. I owe you one."

"And don't think I won't find a way to cash in on that favor, either," he joked. "I'll let you know as soon as I have something."

"Great—thanks." Isaac disconnected the call, feeling certain Nate would come through for him.

Which was a good thing, since the sooner he spoke to Cam Walker, the better.

He headed back inside to join Leah and Ben. She glanced at him questioningly, but he simply smiled without saying anything. There would be plenty of time to talk to her later, once Walker called him back.

"Here's your picture, Mr. Isaac," Ben said.

He took the drawing and grinned. "This is great, Ben. Looks just like me!"

The boy nodded, digging into his chicken tenders with gusto. Isaac's burger and Leah's chicken sandwich had arrived as well, and no one said much as they ate.

When they finished, Isaac paid the bill. As they walked outside, his cell phone rang. Recognizing Nate's number, he quickly answered. "Do you have something?" he asked.

"Yeah, my contact agreed to get a message

to Cameron Walker. I gave him this number to use—hope that's okay."

"It's perfect. Thanks a lot."

"Listen, Isaac, if you need help, let me know, okay?"

He appreciated Nate's willingness to help. It was the same offer Jenna had given him. "I will, Nate. Thanks again."

He clicked off his cell and glanced over at Leah. She'd already helped Ben into his booster seat and was waiting by the car.

"I'm trying to get in touch with your brother's ATF contact," Isaac explained. "This guy should be able to help us find Shane."

"That's wonderful," Leah said, her eyes lighting up with hope. "Maybe our prayers will be answered."

"I'm with you," he agreed. He slid in behind the wheel at the same time Leah climbed in from her side. The trip back to the cabin didn't take long, but from the way Leah kept tapping her feet, he knew she was anxious for Walker to call him.

He was, too, for that matter.

But it wasn't until Leah had given Ben a bath and put him to bed that Isaac's cell phone rang. He noticed the number had a Madison area code, and since that was the capital, it made sense that Walker would live there.

"Hello?"

"Deputy Morrison?" the low voice on the other end of the call asked curtly.

"Yes, this is Deputy Isaac Morrison," he acknowledged. "Is this Cameron Walker?"

"Who gave you my name?" he demanded harshly.

Isaac frowned. This call wasn't going at all the way he'd expected. He decided to get right to the point. "Shane Hawkins gave me your name, and he's in trouble. I need you to help me find him."

There was a long pause. "I'll call you back," Walker said gruffly. And promptly disconnected.

Isaac stared at the phone in shock. What in the world was going on? Why wouldn't Walker talk to him?

Dozens of possible scenarios filtered through his mind—none of them good. He tried to call Walker back, but the call went straight through to voice mail.

Leaving him exactly where he'd started, without a single lead to follow and no way of finding Leah's brother.

TWELVE

Leah didn't sleep well that night. She dreamed about finding Shane dead and woke up with her heart pounding and her cheeks wet with tears. She dragged herself out of bed, glad to see that Isaac had picked up breakfast and already fed Ben.

After they finished eating, the hours dragged by slowly. There were only so many ways to entertain her son. And Isaac was like a caged animal, pacing the small cabin, checking his phone at least a dozen times every hour. She knew he was waiting to hear from Cameron Walker, the ATF agent working with Shane, but had no idea why it was taking so long for him to call back.

By early afternoon, she couldn't stand the tension for another minute. "How about we take Ben to the playground? It would be good to get out of here for a while."

Isaac looked as if he wanted to refuse, but he surprised her by nodding. "Okay, that sounds good."

Ben was ecstatic, jumping up and down between them. She grasped his hand and was taken off guard when Isaac took Ben's other hand. Ben gleefully lifted his feet off the ground, hanging on and swinging back and forth.

Once again, she was struck by the knowledge that anyone watching the three of them making their way down the path to the playground would assume they were a happy family. Leah was stunned to realize the thought didn't fill her with panic the way it might have a few days ago.

She glanced at Isaac from beneath her lashes, thinking once again how handsome he looked. She gave herself a mental shake. Why was she even considering a relationship with him? He could have his pick of any woman on the planet, so there was no reason for him to be interested in a widow with a son. Even if she was ready to try again, which she definitely wasn't.

As soon as the playground was within sight, Ben let go of their hands and ran forward with a whoop.

"Thank goodness it's not raining," she said, tucking a stray curl behind her ear. "That boy needs to burn off some energy."

Isaac smiled, but then frowned as he glanced up at the cloudy sky. "I wouldn't be surprised if we get rain later tonight," he said soberly. "Which could pose a problem when I head out to look for Hawk."

"You mean when *we* go and look for my brother," she corrected.

Isaac simply lifted a brow. "You need to stay here to keep an eye on Ben."

She followed her son's progress as he climbed the monkey bars. Of course she didn't want to place Ben in danger, but if Shane was hurt, her nursing skills might come in handy. "I was thinking about that," she said in a low voice. "What if we asked Caleb and Noelle to watch Ben for a while? He'd be safe with them and would also get a kick out of spending time with Kaitlin. They really bonded in the swimming pool."

Isaac's lips firmed in a thin line. "A better idea is for you to go with Ben to stay with Caleb and Noelle."

"What if Shane is hurt?" she pressed. "I want to help him, the way he helped me after Elliot died."

Isaac shook his head, but then shrugged. "We'll see what happens once I hear from Walker. And I'm getting worried, since he hasn't phoned or returned any of my calls. I don't like it."

She didn't like it, either.

And even though she tried not to think about the worst-case scenario, the images kept flitting through her mind. All she could do was put her faith in God.

* * *

Isaac scrubbed his hands over his face, the sick feeling in his gut getting worse with every minute that passed. Okay, maybe it made sense for Cam Walker to do a little digging into his background before trusting him, but certainly it wouldn't take this long. Not with the resources the ATF had at their disposal.

Once they returned to the cabin, he stoked the fire to get rid of the chill in the air. When his phone rang, he dropped the poker and hurried to pick up the call, fearing Walker wouldn't give him much time. "Yeah?"

"I'm not happy Hawk gave you my name," Cam said in lieu of a greeting. "He wasn't supposed to tell anyone about this op."

Isaac didn't like the guy's attitude. "Yeah, well, he's in trouble, so I don't really care."

There was a long pause. "How do you know he's in trouble?"

"Because you know as well as I do that his cover is blown," Isaac said curtly. "And there are dirty cops involved, aren't there?"

"Yeah, that's what we believe, although we don't have any proof," Walker admitted.

"You must have someone at the top of the suspect list?" Isaac pressed.

Another pause. "Two names—Trey Birchwood and Aaron Winslow."

Isaac frowned, not quite understanding why Hawk hadn't informed Cameron about Trey's murder. But he wasn't going to say anything if his buddy hadn't. And Aaron Winslow was the same suspect Hawk had identified as well, the guy who'd *claimed* his car was stolen.

Unfortunately, poking into Winslow's background hadn't turned up anything suspicious.

"Good to know," Isaac said.

"When's the last time you heard from Hawk?" Cameron asked.

"Yesterday early afternoon," he admitted. "Do you have any idea where we can find him?"

"He's been moving around a lot, but I think he's been hiding in an abandoned shed located in a small town called Hanover, outside the city."

"Have you been there to meet with him?" Isaac demanded. He couldn't understand why the ATF agent wasn't doing more to help Hawk.

"I'm heading there now, but I'm a good hour away," Cameron responded. "Why don't you meet me there? Maybe between the two of us we'll be able to figure out where he might have gone."

"I will. Give me the closest cross street." He quickly jotted down the information Walker gave him. "I'll meet you there in an hour."

Isaac quickly called Caleb. "I need to drop off Leah and Ben for a couple of hours, if that's okay."

"Sure. We're having movie night and I know Kaitlin will be happy to spend time with Ben."

He could feel Leah's gaze boring into his chest, but he wasn't in the mood to argue. "Thanks. Be there shortly."

Leah was already dressed in jeans and a dark sweatshirt, and she was putting Ben's coat on before Isaac even finished the call. But once they were settled in the car, she glared at him. "I'm going with you," she said. "Don't bother wasting your breath to try and stop me."

He scowled and tried to think of a way to make her see reason. "I'll be able to move faster on my own," he pointed out.

She crossed her arms over her chest and he sighed when he recognized the stubborn look on her face. "Why haven't you called Declan to go along?"

"Deck hasn't gotten back to me, so I'm assuming he's busy with something else. And I don't need anyone else with me. I'll be working with the ATF agent."

"Fine. You and the ATF agent can do all the work. I'll just be there to provide any medical help Shane needs."

Isaac couldn't deny that having her nursing skills available might come in handy. But on the other hand, if Hawk was dead, he'd end up placing Leah in danger for no good reason.

Glancing over at her, he knew he couldn't point out that part. Better for her to have hope, at least until they knew the truth.

When he pulled up in front of Caleb's house, she didn't move to get out of the vehicle. No way was he going to convince her to stay, short of using a sandblaster to pry her out of the car.

"Okay, fine. You can come along, but you're going to do everything I say, agreed?"

"Agreed."

Caleb strode out to meet them, and Isaac climbed out and helped Ben get down from his booster seat. "'Bye, Mom," he yelled before running off to meet up with Kaitlin.

"Thanks, Caleb," Isaac said in a low tone. "I'll be in touch as soon as possible."

"No worries, we'll be fine," his teammate assured him before turning to walk back inside.

Isaac didn't waste any time getting to the intersection Walker had given him. Dusk had fallen early, thanks to the dark clouds looming overhead.

"We're looking for a dirt road," he said to Leah.

"Is that it?" she said, gesturing to a space between some trees. The road started out okay, but up ahead he could see two deep ruts in the mud.

No way was the car going to handle that. He drove forward, glad to see there was a small clearing off to the right, just large enough to park the car. He pulled forward, the low-hanging tree branches scraping the top of the car. When they fell over the back window, offering a bit of coverage, he stopped and turned off the engine.

"I want you to stay here," he said, handing Leah the car keys. "And if anything goes wrong, you get out of here and head back to Caleb's house."

She opened her mouth to argue, but then closed it again without saying a word. He was glad she planned to adhere to her side of the bargain.

He opened his door, but then turned back to give her a quick kiss. The stunned expression on her face made him smile as he ducked outside, softly closing the door behind him.

But as he moved through the trees, avoiding the muddy drive, he kept his gun close at hand, ready for anything.

He wasn't sure exactly where this abandoned shed was located, so he tried to follow the general direction indicated by the muddy ruts. But when he noticed a dark shape looming to the right, he turned in that direction.

The dilapidated building looked like an abandoned shed. He crouched near a large tree, looking for any sign of life. Of course there was nothing.

He didn't want to believe that was because Hawk was already dead. Pushing the dire thought away, Isaac debated what to do. He didn't see any sign of the ATF agent. Granted, he was a little early, so maybe Walker had run into traffic on the way here.

After waiting a minute, Isaac decided to make his move. At the very least he needed to make sure that Hawk wasn't lying on the floor inside, injured or worse. Staying low, he ran over to the corner closest to the door, which was hanging half-open on one rusty hinge.

He quickly slid inside the shed, nearly choking on the rank, musty smell that filled the place. He waited for his eyes to adjust to the darkness, but when he still couldn't see well enough, he pulled out his phone and cupped his hand over the screen to provide a sliver of light.

The shed was empty. But as he swept his gaze about, he could see there were scuff marks on the floor, as if someone might have been hiding there. Stepping farther into the building, he discovered there was an old army blanket stuffed in a corner.

And a dark, rusty smear on the edge of a wooden plank that might have been blood.

Isaac stood and made his way back toward the half-open shed door. Hawk had definitely been hiding out here at one time.

But where was he now?

Leah huddled in the corner of the passenger seat, trying to keep warm. No sense in complaining, since it was her own fault that she'd come along.

The area around her appeared to be deserted. She eased the passenger door open and climbed out so she could walk around to get her blood moving.

Besides, she should sit in the driver's seat in case she had to leave in a hurry.

The air outside the car was cool and breezy, but having room to move around helped. She did a series of high steps as silently as possible, feeling much warmer afterward.

Anxious to know what was going on, she crept through the brush with painstaking slowness, trying not to make any noise. She caught a glimpse of the abandoned shed and hunkered down to watch.

Not that it was easy to see much in the darkness. Out here there were no street lamps for miles. The dark clouds obliterated any potential light from the stars and moon.

There was a sudden flash of light beyond the shed, in the clearing behind it. Her pulse leaped at the possibility that the light had something to do with her brother. Was he trying to signal for help?

She stayed where she was, even though every cell in her body wanted nothing more than to rush over to see if that light was connected to Shane. But the potential that she might be wrong kept her rooted in place.

Her legs eventually ached from the uncomfortable position, but she did her best to ignore it. She remembered the first night she'd met Isaac, when the Jeep tire had been blown out. So much had happened since then, yet amazingly enough, the time could be measured in days.

A few days, yet it seemed like a lifetime ago.

She saw the flash of light again and caught a glimpse of a man before darkness surrounded him once more. She'd seen the guy's face for only barest of seconds, but knew he seemed familiar. She followed the dark figure as he moved through the area, hoping and praying he'd flash his light again.

The next time he did, the man's features clicked in her memory. He looked like Kirk Nash, Shane's boss, from the Fifth District.

She frowned. Why would Lieutenant Nash be out here in the darkness? What was he searching for? She didn't understand, but somehow knew that something wasn't right.

A movement near the shed caught her attention and she sucked in a harsh breath when she recognized Isaac creeping along the side of the building. He must have noticed the flickering light, too, and she wished there was a way to warn him about Nash. But calling his cell would only put him in danger.

Plus he'd be upset if he knew she was so close, so she eased back, retracing her steps to hide farther back in the woods, since she couldn't bring herself to go all the way to the car.

She needed to trust that Isaac knew what he was doing. He wasn't part of the SWAT team for nothing. If there was a way for him to find Shane and bring him back, he would.

So Leah silently prayed for strength and patience.

Isaac peered around the corner of the shed, waiting for the flash of light to return. He'd noticed it when he happened to glance at the right moment through the open window.

There it was again! It was so quick he might have missed it if he'd blinked.

But there was no doubt about it—someone was out there. Hawk? Or Cameron Walker?

It occurred to Isaac that he didn't know what Cam Walker looked like. What if the guy out there wasn't Walker at all? What if the dirty cops had been tipped off about the location of the shed? They could right now be out there waiting to ambush him.

He took a deep breath to calm his racing pulse. There was no way to know if the person out there with the light was friend or foe. And he didn't plan to show himself until he knew for sure one way or the other.

It was hard to imagine why Cameron would

have lured him here. Maybe they thought that if they captured him, they'd have leverage with Hawk? But that would mean Cameron Walker was dirty, and Isaac wasn't quite ready to go there yet.

The next flash was closer, and he caught enough of a glimpse to realize the guy was looking down in the brush. Was he searching for a blood trail?

The tiny hairs on the back of Isaac's neck lifted in alarm. Something about this whole scenario didn't seem right. If the guy out there was Cameron Walker, why didn't he say something?

Whoever he was, he was making his way closer to the shed. Maybe he was Cameron Walker and maybe he wasn't, but somehow Isaac didn't think he should stick around long enough to find out.

Especially since there was no sign of Hawk.

Isaac went in the opposite direction, keeping the shed between himself and the other man. He needed to get back to the car and take off before this guy realized he'd ever been here.

Moving silently through the woods wasn't easy. He didn't dare go too fast, though everything in his body urged him to get back to Leah as soon as possible.

He neared the area where he thought he'd left the car, but didn't see it. Had he gone too far?

After making another sweep of the area, he

spotted it, closer to the main road than he remembered. As he approached, he didn't see Leah inside and his chest squeezed with fear. Had someone taken her?

The sound of a twig snapping to his left had him swiveling around, his gun drawn. Every ounce of tension drained from his body when he recognized Leah.

"Isaac," she whispered, stumbling toward him. "Did you see him?"

"Let's get in the car," he whispered back, unwilling to have this conversation out where the man in the woods could still find them.

She nodded and pressed the keys into his hand. Opening and closing the car door seemed unusually loud, and once they were both safe inside, he jammed the key into the ignition, started the engine and took off.

There wasn't a moment to waste. He wanted to put as much distance between them and the guy back there as possible.

Leah must have sensed the seriousness of the situation because she didn't say a word until a good ten minutes had passed.

"Do you think he's following us?" she asked, craning around in her seat to peer out the back window.

"Not yet," he answered grimly. "I almost had

a heart attack when I saw you hiding in the trees. Why didn't you stay in the car like I asked?"

"Don't yell at me, okay? I know I shouldn't have gone out there, but I'm glad I did. Did you see that guy searching the clearing around the shed with his light?"

"Yeah, I saw him. I'm sure it was the ATF agent, Cameron Walker."

"No, it wasn't," she corrected. "I managed to get a glimpse of his face and I recognized him. He's Lieutenant Kirk Nash, Shane's boss."

"Are you sure?" Isaac demanded.

"I'm sure. I've met him before." Leah sounded positive and he had no reason to doubt her.

Before he could ask more questions, there was a low groan from the rear of the sedan. The sound was so unexpected, he jerked the steering wheel sharply, nearly running them off the road.

Someone was back there!

THIRTEEN

Leah's heart leaped into her throat as she swiveled to peer into the backseat.

"Get down," Isaac said harshly. He pulled over to the side of the road and abruptly stopped the car.

Leah ignored him, using her phone as a flashlight so she could see better. "Shane?" she asked incredulously. "How did you get in here?"

"I crawled," he said before letting out another low groan. "Good thing I saw you."

"What's wrong? What happened? Are you hurt?" Leah could hardly believe her brother was here, after all this time. And from what she could tell, not a moment too soon. Shane looked awful.

"Wait a minute! Hawk? Is that really you?" Isaac had opened the back door and was standing there, holding his gun ready.

"Yeah. Took a hit—in my shoulder."

"Let me see." Leah quickly got out of the car and came around to where Isaac was standing, clearly dumbfounded. "I need to take a look at his wound."

"Not now," Shane protested in a low voice. "Keep driving. Need to get away."

Leah ignored him, although it wasn't easy to climb into the backseat with her brother sprawled half on and half off the cushions.

"He's right, Leah," Isaac said. "We need to get out of here."

No way was she leaving her brother's side. "I'm staying back here."

Isaac sighed and muttered, "Fine" before he closed the door after her and slid back behind the wheel. Within seconds he had the car on the road again.

Leah couldn't see much in the darkness, but just being near her brother brought a level of comfort. Ever since she'd heard him cry out in pain on the other end of the phone, she'd secretly feared the worst.

"Where's your wound?" she asked, bracing herself on the seat. "We need to apply pressure to minimize the blood loss."

"Left shoulder," he said with a grunt. "Bleeding seems to have slowed down."

She felt along his left side, following his arm up to his shoulder. When she felt beneath his jacket, she found the fabric of his shirt hardened with dried blood. She noticed he was shaking and understood that he was in shock, either from blood loss, infection or both.

"Isaac, will you crank the heat?" she asked, shrugging out of her sweatshirt. She was glad it was dark as she quickly stripped off the T-shirt she was wearing underneath before putting her sweatshirt back on.

"Sure. How is he?"

"Hanging in there," she responded, pressing her balled-up shirt against her brother's shoulder. Gunshot wounds were nothing to play around with. "We need to get him to a hospital as soon as possible."

"No hospital," Shane said, reaching out to grasp her arm with a strength that surprised her. "I mean it, Leah—no hospital."

"Look, I know gunshot wounds have to be reported to the police," she said. "But I promise I won't leave you alone."

"Doesn't matter," he mumbled. He was beginning to slur his words and she hated seeing him like this. "They'll try to pin this all on me."

"Shane, if you don't get medical help soon, you could die," she said. "You need antibiotics, fluids, maybe even a blood transfusion. I can't provide all that for you."

"Even more people could die if I don't stop the person in charge of this mess," Shane said. "Please, Leah, you have to trust me. No hospital."

"Let's get back to the cabin first," Isaac said, clearly trying to play the peacemaker. "Once you can see the full extent of Hawk's injuries, we'll decide our next steps."

Leah grimaced and nodded, feeling helpless. They could try going to a hospital that wasn't located in Milwaukee, but she knew that the doctors there would only transfer Shane to the closest level-one trauma center, which happened to be smack in the middle of the Milwaukee Police Department district. The only other one was over two hours away, and even they might transfer him regardless.

The only other option was to bring a physician to her brother. A physician and supplies.

As she turned the idea around in her mind, Leah thought of just the person who might be willing to do her a favor.

"Isaac, I need to make a call." She grasped the back of Isaac's seat as he took a sharp right. "Will you hand me my phone?"

"Depends. Who are you calling?" he demanded. "I don't think we should ignore your brother's concern about going to the hospital."

"I know, but I want to call a trauma-doctor friend of mine. I'm pretty sure she'll help us."

Isaac captured Leah's gaze in the rearview mirror. "Being friends is one thing. Breaking the law is something entirely different. I highly doubt this doctor will be willing to come remove a bullet without notifying the police."

"You don't know Dr. Gabriella Fielding," she responded. "I think she'll come, because last month I helped her out when we had a meth addict go crazy in the middle of the trauma bay."

"What do you mean?" Isaac demanded. "How exactly did you help her?"

Leah nibbled her lower lip, remembering that night all too well. "Our patient leaped off the trauma table, grabbed a scalpel and charged toward her. I shoved a bedside tray in front of him and then stomped on his hand to get the scalpel. He tossed me on my backside, but thankfully, the security guards took over from there, managing to hold him still enough that we could sedate him."

"You never told me that," Shane said. The light from the moon was barely enough to see his troubled gaze.

Leah winced and nodded. "I know. I didn't want you to worry. Honestly, it all happened so fast, I don't even remember making a conscious decision to do anything."

"And you think my job is dangerous," Isaac muttered. He shook his head. "The cabin is only a few miles away, in any case. Why don't you wait to see what you're dealing with before you call her?"

He had a point, especially since they were so

close to the cabin. Leah felt certain Gabby would help, if she wasn't working.

And if she was, then Leah would just have to do her best to treat Shane until Gabby could get there.

Isaac was relieved to make it back to the cabin without a problem. He'd purposefully taken a long, winding route just to be sure they hadn't been followed. The entire fiasco at the shed still didn't sit well with him and he hoped Hawk would stay conscious until help arrived.

Getting Hawk into the cabin was no small feat. "You take his injured side. I'll take the other," he instructed Leah.

"Okay," she agreed.

Hawk was weak, and even with Leah's help, Isaac had to practically drag him inside. Since the sofa was closer than a bedroom, he headed in that direction, getting him there just as his friend's legs collapsed beneath him. He groaned as he landed with a thud.

"Sorry, man," Isaac exclaimed.

"Shane, are you all right?" Leah was leaning over him, her serious expression betraying the depth of her concern.

"Call your doctor friend," Isaac told her. "I'll help get him undressed enough so you can look at his wound."

Leah pressed her lips together as if she was near tears, but nodded and stepped away to make the call. He knelt on the floor beside Hawk and tugged at his jacket.

"What happened out there tonight, Hawk?" he asked in a low tone as he worked.

For a moment he thought his buddy was too far gone to answer, but then he opened his eyes. "The shed was my hiding spot, but they found me. So I took off and hid in the woods."

Isaac noticed Hawk winced when he tried to slip his injured arm out of the sleeve. He was trying to be gentle, but the blood-soaked clothing didn't give way easily. "You were shot yesterday, though, right?"

"Yeah, but I wasn't at the shed then. I was about ten miles down the road."

"Ten miles?" Isaac was shocked to hear that. "How did you manage to go ten miles without a vehicle?"

"It wasn't easy." Hawk closed his eyes and groaned again. "Took me forever, since I had to stay hidden the whole time."

"So how did they find you at the shed?" Isaac asked, trying to understand the chain of events.

"I knew I needed to keep going, but I must have passed out for a bit. When I came to, it was getting dark and I knew that they might find me. So

I contacted Cam Walker. Told him where I was hiding and that I needed help."

That made sense, considering the timing of the ATF agent's phone call. "I was supposed to meet Walker there an hour after we talked," Isaac stated grimly. "Sounds like he contacted me as soon as he heard from you."

"He called you?" Confusion darkened Hawk's eyes, which were the same shade of blue as Leah's. "I don't understand. He never showed up."

A sick feeling lodged in Isaac's gut. "So that wasn't Walker looking for you in the woods?" he asked carefully. "Because Leah thought the guy out there was your boss, Lieutenant Nash."

"She's right," Hawk said grimly. "The minute I saw him, I knew I had to get out of there."

"You think he's involved?" Isaac asked.

His friend hesitated and then shook his head. "I honestly don't know. Either he's in on the whole illegal gunrunning deal or someone else is feeding him wrong information. The guy I thought was involved was Aaron Winslow."

Made sense, since the stolen car belonged to Winslow, and Cameron had believed Winslow was guilty, too. Although maybe Cam had only heard that from Hawk?

Isaac's instincts were to believe the worst. He knew from what Caleb had been through last year that even the top brass could wallow in the mud, getting their badges dirty. Being the rank of lieutenant didn't mean squat if enough money was involved.

"Isaac, is it okay if I give Gabby directions to the cabin?" Leah asked.

"Yeah, it's fine." What choice did they have? Now that he had Hawk's shirt off, he saw that the bullet wound in his shoulder was far worse than he'd anticipated. And there wasn't an exit wound, which meant the slug was still embedded in his shoulder.

The doctor might be able to help stabilize Hawk temporarily, but Isaac didn't see how they would manage to avoid sending him to the hospital, sooner or later.

He could only hope that they'd break the case open before they had to take that chance.

Leah was relieved that Gabriella wasn't working and had agreed to come help take care of Shane. The trauma surgeon was bringing a bunch of supplies as well, including IV antibiotics.

Isaac had gotten Shane's jacket and shirt off, but his shoulder was a mess, so she headed into the kitchen to fill a bowl with hot water.

"What do you want to do about Ben?" Isaac asked from the fireplace, where he was building a roaring blaze.

"He's safe with Caleb for now, isn't he? I think

we need to make sure Shane gets the help he needs before we go pick him up."

"All right," Isaac agreed. "I'll let Caleb know to keep Ben there overnight. I'm sure he won't mind."

"Thanks." She carried the water to the sofa and then brought over the stack of towels she'd taken from the bathroom. Shane's eyes were closed, but as much as she hated to bother him, she needed to clean his wound.

"Sorry, this might hurt a bit," she said as she gently pressed the warm washcloth over the area.

Shane flinched but didn't open his eyes, and she hoped he was simply sleeping and hadn't fallen unconscious.

The water turned a dark rusty-brown by the time she finished her task. And the skin around the opening looked red and puffy, a sure sign it was infected.

Leah rocked back on her heels, second-guessing her decision to go along with Shane's wishes. Maybe she should have insisted on taking her brother to the hospital.

If she hadn't caught that glimpse of Shane's boss out there in the clearing by the shed, she wouldn't have been as worried. But she had, and now she didn't have the faintest idea of whom they could trust.

She found a small package of gauze in the bathroom cabinet, no doubt left by a previous renter, and she placed it over the wound and then layered blankets over her brother to keep him warm.

While they waited for Gabby to arrive, Leah tried to get her brother to drink some broth she'd found in the cupboard, likely from the previous occupants. He took only a few sips before turning away.

Finally, she heard the sound of a car engine pulling up out front. Leah darted toward the door, but Isaac beat her to it, holding his weapon ready as he peered outside.

"Dr. Fielding?" Isaac asked in a low voice.

"Yes, it's me. Is Leah there?"

There was a hint of fear in her friend's tone, so Leah pushed Isaac aside to open the door. "I'm here, Gabby, and this is Deputy Isaac Morrison. Thank you so much for coming."

"Not a problem, since my social life is nonexistent. Besides, I owe you a favor," Gabby said with a wry smile. "Sorry it took me so long, but this place wasn't easy to find even with your directions."

"Here, let me help you with that," Isaac said, taking the large backpack she had slung over her shoulder.

"Thanks. Where's my patient?"

"Over here on the sofa. I cleaned his wound as best I could," Leah said. "But it still looks pretty bad. And I tried to get some fluids into him, too, but didn't have much luck."

"Hmm…" Gabby knelt beside Shane's prone figure. "You mentioned the bullet has been embedded inside his shoulder for over twenty-four hours?"

"At least—maybe a little longer," she confirmed.

"Not good. Is there any way to get him into one of the bedrooms? It's going to be too difficult to work on him here."

Isaac grimaced, but nodded. "I'll do my best."

"Shane? Can you help us by getting up?" Leah asked, giving her brother a small shake. "Come on. We need you to stretch out on one of the beds."

His eyelids fluttered open, and for a moment he looked confused, but then his expression cleared. "I'll try."

It took the three of them working together to haul Shane into the closest bedroom.

"Okay, first we need to start the IV fluids and antibiotics," Gabby said, digging through her backpack. "You said he doesn't have any known allergies, right?"

Leah nodded. "None that I know of."

"Okay, good. Once we have that done, I'll need to remove the bullet from the wound or it will fester and make the infection worse."

Leah nodded again. Gabriella's plan was exactly what she'd expected. "What can I do to help?"

"Why don't you start the IV while I get things set up. I'm going to need better lighting, too."

"I'll bring both lamps from the living room," Isaac said, obviously anxious to assist.

"Thanks." Gabby barely spared him a glance, her attention focused solely on her patient.

Leah's fingers were shaking as she started the IV in her brother's arm. She tried to tell herself this was just like being in the trauma room.

But it wasn't.

Once the fluids and antibiotics were infusing, Gabby gave Shane a non-narcotic painkiller. Leah didn't ask why she hadn't brought along narcotics. There was a limit to what Gabby would do, Leah knew, and taking narcotics without accounting for them wasn't one of them, since discrepancies had to be reported to the DEA. Quite honestly, she didn't blame Gabby one bit.

"Ready?" her friend asked, meeting her gaze.

Leah nodded. They both had sterile gloves on, even though the cabin was hardly a pristine environment. Still, Gabby had brought more supplies than Leah had expected, including sterile drapes and several surgical instruments. Leah picked up the two small retractors and gently held the edges of the wound open.

Shane flinched and gritted his teeth, but didn't protest as Gabby probed the wound as gently as possible with a forceps. Retrieving the bullet actually didn't take long at all, but she spent a lot of time flushing out the wound with an antibiotic solution before packing it with sterile gauze.

Finally the surgeon straightened, putting a hand against her lower back as she stretched her sore muscles. "That's all I can do for now," she said in a weary tone. "We can only hope it's enough."

Leah nodded and finished dressing the wound. "I hope so, too. Thanks so much for coming out here and bringing all the supplies."

"No problem." Gabby glanced down at Shane. "I don't suppose you want to tell me why you didn't take him to the hospital?"

Leah grimaced. Her friend deserved to know something after what she'd just done to save his life. "My brother is a cop and his boss might have been the one to blow his cover, causing him to be shot. Seemed safer to do it this way until we know more."

"I understand," Gabby said. "But how, exactly, are you going to find out the truth about his boss?"

Good question. Too bad Leah didn't have an equally good answer. She hadn't thought past getting Shane the medical treatment he needed. But

now that he'd been taken care of, she realized that
they were right back where they'd started from.

They still didn't know whom to trust.

FOURTEEN

Isaac listened to the women's conversation with a sense of helplessness. Gabby wasn't a cop but she'd easily identified the main issue facing them. Hawk was safe, but they still needed to figure out whom to trust and where to go from here. Not that Isaac's friend would be going anywhere anytime soon. Clearly, he needed some rest and nourishment after being on the run for so long.

Dr. Gabby gathered her things together and left them alone. Leah swayed on her feet, looking wiped out.

"Why don't you get some rest?" Isaac suggested. "I'll keep an eye on your brother."

"Not yet," Leah protested. "I need to make sure that he gets his next dose of IV antibiotics in roughly…" she squinted at her watch "…four hours. At three in the morning."

"I'll wake you up then," Isaac said sternly. "You won't be any good to him if you fall apart from lack of sleep."

She let out a sigh and nodded. "All right, but not until I get him to drink more broth."

The stubborn glint was back in her eye, reminding Isaac of the way Hawk used to get when he was convinced he was right and everyone else was wrong. Arguing was useless, so he turned away and grabbed his phone to send Caleb a text message. The time was just after eleven, too late for a phone call, but he sent a message hoping his teammate would look at his phone first thing in the morning.

Then Isaac dropped down in front of the computer, trying to rub the exhaustion from his eyes. The broth Leah heated up for her brother smelled good, and he decided to make a cup for himself, too.

He sipped the warm liquid, pondering the computer screen. The answer had to be connected with Wade Sharkey and Joey Stainwhite. In fact, he'd hoped to have Stainwhite in custody by now. Setting his mug aside, Isaac tapped on the keys to pull up their respective mug shots. He stared at the two men thoughtfully. They were selling illegal weapons, guns that couldn't be traced by the serial number, obviously for profit. Perfect type of weapon to use for committing a crime, like the mall shooting incident, as it made the gun much more difficult to trace. And either Stan's Liquor

Store or some similar place was where they handled their so-called business transactions.

It made sense, if you were into that sort of thing. And he could see how the two guys had earned themselves reputations as a source for untraceable guns.

But he had to think bigger. Why would Sharkey and Stainwhite need contacts within the police department? Was it because one of the cops, maybe Aaron Winslow, had stumbled across their scheme and wanted a piece of the pie for himself? And if so, how was Lieutenant Nash involved, if at all? Or was there something more going on?

Abruptly, Isaac straightened as a thought popped into his head. What if the police department itself was a source for illegal guns? He knew firsthand how dozens of weapons were confiscated from crime scenes every week. They were saved as evidence for trial, but once a perp pleaded out, they were simply stored in boxes. Who would notice if a few went missing? Especially once the serial numbers were removed?

Isaac's pulse leaped with excitement. The Fifth District was in the middle of the city, an area with the highest crime rate. The cops who worked there must confiscate hundreds of weapons a month.

As he turned the idea over in his mind, he knew he was onto something. Every instinct in his body screamed that he was on the right track, but obviously he needed proof. Going to Griff Vaughn with his idea wasn't an option at this point. He'd asked Jenna to follow up with the ballistics on the gun from the mall shooting, but maybe they hadn't gone back far enough. If they could prove that the gun had been used in another crime located within the Fifth District of Milwaukee, then he'd have more of a connection to investigate. A connection that could potentially lead to the proof he desperately needed.

He was tempted to call Jenna right now, but it was late enough that he decided to go with a simple text message. Call me when you have time, Isaac.

Drumming his fingers on the table, his previous exhaustion having vanished, he tried to think of another angle to work. Finding out if Hawk's contact within the ATF, Cam Walker, had the same theory would help, but he wasn't willing to call the guy, not after the way things had gone down at the abandoned shed.

Would Hawk know what Cam's theory was? Maybe. Isaac pushed away from the computer and headed into the bedroom he'd given up for Hawk. He stopped in the doorway when he saw Leah sitting in a chair beside her brother's bed, her head cradled in her arms, apparently sound asleep. Hawk looked to be sleeping, too, and for a moment Isaac considered waking him up to discuss his theory. But his buddy's pale skin and the fresh bandage on his shoulder convinced him to wait until morning.

But he couldn't bear to leave Leah sitting there in such an awkward position. She'd wake up with a backache for sure. He crossed over and gently squeezed her shoulder. "Leah," he whispered. "Come on. You need to get some sleep."

"What?" She blinked groggily at him and then sat up with a wince. "What time is it?"

"Almost one in the morning," he whispered. "Get to bed. I'll wake you up in a few hours so you can administer the antibiotic."

"Okay." It was a testament to how tired she was that she didn't argue. He supported her with a hand under her arm as she staggered to her feet. She leaned heavily against him as they made their way into the second bedroom, the one she shared with Ben.

"Isaac?" She stood there, clutching his arm, and all he could remember was how sweet she'd tasted when he'd kissed her. How much he wanted to kiss her again.

Not now, Morrison, he told himself sternly.

"What? Do you need something?" he asked.

"I— Nothing. Thank you, for everything."

He sensed that wasn't really what she had been about to say, but since her eyes were half-closed, he didn't push it.

"You're welcome. Get some sleep." He helped her sit on the edge of the mattress, moving back to give her room.

"G'night," she mumbled as she crawled into bed fully dressed. She closed her eyes and didn't move, so he backed out of the room and softly closed the door behind him.

He blew out a heavy breath, wishing he'd asked her how to give the IV antibiotic so he wouldn't have to wake her at all, but it was too late now. He didn't want to make things worse by trying to figure it out on his own.

Isaac headed back to the kitchen table and tried to think of a good way to pass the next two hours. Unfortunately, he was limited as to what he could do from here.

Just as his eyes started to drift closed, his cell phone rang. He jerked awake. "Morrison," he said, covering up a wide yawn.

"I just got your text message. What's up?" Jenna asked.

He was surprised she'd called him so late, but he was glad to have something concrete to do. "Remember that gun from the mall shooting?"

"Yeah. What about it?"

"How far back did you go as far as testing the ballistics reports?"

"Just a couple of months—why? What's going

on?" She sounded eager to help, which eased his guilt for contacting her so late.

"I have a hunch but need proof. I'd like you to go back further, say a year or maybe even two. I think this gun has been used in another crime." He didn't want to give her too much information, because he wanted to see what she came up with. If he told her to just look in the Fifth District, she might miss something important.

For all he knew, other districts could be involved.

"All right, but you'd better fill me in and soon," Jenna said, sounding testy. "I'm capable of doing more than your menial labor."

"I know you are, and trust me, this isn't menial labor." He didn't know why Jenna was always determined to prove herself, but right now he was too tired to care. "Look, I would do the check from here if I could. I need your help, Jenna. If you want me to call someone else, I will."

"I'll do it," she muttered. "I'll let you know when I have something."

"Thanks. I appreciate it." Isaac disconnected from the call and sighed.

Ninety minutes and he could wake up Leah to administer the antibiotic, and then he'd get some sleep.

He had a feeling that by the morning he'd have a lot more information to work with. And maybe he could talk to Hawk, too, come up with some sort of plan.

Because Leah and Ben weren't safe yet. Not by a long shot. And they wouldn't be safe until he found and arrested the dirty cop responsible for murdering Trey Birchwood and attempting to murder Hawk.

Isaac knew Leah was relieved to have found her brother, and so was he. But right now, the moment of peace felt too much like the calm before the storm.

And he was determined that Leah and Ben would survive, unscathed.

Leah woke up the next morning and bolted upright in bed. Had she overslept? Shane needed another dose of antibiotic at nine o'clock.

She dragged a hand through her hair, attempting to restore some order to her unruly curls, and climbed out of bed, mortified to realize she'd slept in her clothes. As much as she desperately wanted to shower and change, she went to check on Shane.

Following the enticing aroma of coffee, she headed to the main room. She was surprised to see Isaac was up, since he'd gone to bed well after she had. She only vaguely remembered him waking her to give Shane his three o'clock medication.

"Hey, how are you feeling?" Isaac asked when he saw her.

"Good. I'm just going to check on Shane."

"He's doing okay," Isaac said, rising to his feet and crossing to meet her by Shane's doorway. "I gave him more soup about thirty minutes ago."

"Really? How much did he drink?"

"All of it," Isaac said with a grin. "He's been asking for more than broth, but I told him we had to check with you first."

"I'm sure he can have something more," she agreed.

She entered Shane's bedroom, relieved to note that her brother looked much better. She placed a hand on his forehead, satisfied when he didn't feel too warm.

Thankfully, the fluids and antibiotics were doing their job.

"I hear you're hungry," she said.

"I am. I honestly can't tell you the last time I've eaten," Shane confessed. "At least two days ago."

Her heart squeezed in her chest, but she kept a smile on her face. "Okay, how about some scrambled eggs and toast?" She glanced at Isaac. "Maybe we could get a take-out order from the diner?"

"Good plan," he agreed. "Tell me what you want, too, and I'll get enough for all of us."

"How about four servings of scrambled eggs,

toast, bacon and juice?" she suggested. "Leftovers wouldn't be the worst thing in the world. And Ben might be hungry when he gets here."

"Caleb promised to drop him off in about an hour, and I'm pretty sure he'll feed Ben breakfast beforehand," Isaac said. "But I'll get more than enough, just in case."

She nodded and turned back to Shane. "I'm so glad you're doing better," she said in a low tone. "You have no idea how worried I've been."

"Hey, I've been worried about you, too," he said, grimacing when he shifted in the bed. "I'm glad Ice has been here to look after you."

"It's almost time for your next dose of antibiotic, but after that we can see about letting you get cleaned up a bit. No shower, though. We can't let your shoulder wound get wet."

Shane frowned but didn't argue. She actually couldn't blame him for wanting a shower.

"How much has Ice told you?" he inquired, changing the subject as she prepared the antibiotic infusion.

"What do you mean?" she asked, perplexed. "I know everything that's been going on."

"Really?" Her brother looked surprised.

"Why wouldn't I know? Isaac has been with me ever since the masked man tried to kidnap me and Ben."

"I guess I assumed you wouldn't want to know

any of the details," Shane admitted. "You never wanted to know anything about the dangerous aspects of my job before."

Since he was right, she couldn't very well argue. She concentrated on hanging the IV medication and then turned to sit beside his bed.

"I'm sorry about that," she said in a low tone. "I realize now how foolish I've been. Refusing to listen to the details of your job certainly didn't make it less dangerous. And as a trauma nurse I see gunshot and stab victims being brought in all the time. I guess it was a stupid way to try and cope."

"Not stupid," he corrected, reaching out to take her hand. "I understand how hard it must be for you to know that I'm out on the streets doing the same job our father did."

She gripped his hand tightly and nodded. "It was hard, but that doesn't mean I don't owe you a huge apology. It was selfish of me to think only about myself. I should have realized how much support you needed, too. I'm embarrassed to admit that it took hearing you got hurt to make me realize what I was doing."

"Hey, you don't have to apologize to me," Shane protested. "I hated knowing how afraid you were for me. But this is the job I'm meant to do, Leah. I thought about changing careers for you, but I couldn't do it. Well," he amended, "I could, but I wouldn't be happy."

It struck her at that moment how much Isaac was the same way. He was obviously a great cop and valued being a part of the SWAT team. How could she ever expect him to do anything else?

Very simply, she couldn't. And he shouldn't have to change who he was or what he did for anyone.

Least of all for her.

Truthfully, she didn't want to change who he was. Over these past few days she'd needed him to keep her and Ben safe, which included taking advantage of all his cop skills.

And why was she even thinking about being with Isaac once this was all done? Other than that amazing kiss, he'd never given her any indication that he wanted to see her on a personal level.

So why couldn't she get the idea out of her mind?

"Mommy!" Ben came rushing into the bedroom and she turned and scooped him up in a huge hug.

"Oh, I missed you," she murmured against his neck. He smelled like baby shampoo, and she was so glad that he'd missed last night's events.

"Uncle Shane! You're here!" Ben wiggled to indicate he wanted to get down.

"Easy now—Uncle Shane has a big ouchie in

his shoulder," she cautioned as she set her son on his feet.

"What happened?" Ben nimbly climbed onto the bed and crawled up beside Shane. "Did someone stab you?"

Oh, boy, since when did Ben get so bloodthirsty? "No, he wasn't stabbed," she corrected. "But his ouchie is infected, so we have to be very careful."

"I missed you," Ben said, resting his head against Shane's right side.

Her brother hugged him close and smiled. "I know, buddy. I missed you, too."

Leah had to look away, blinking the tears from her eyes. She should be happy. The outcome could have been so much worse.

"Hey, Ben, why don't you show your mom your new toy?" Isaac suggested from the doorway. "I need to talk to Uncle Shane for a few minutes."

"Okay. Come on, Mom—look at what Mr. Caleb bought for me." Ben scrambled off the bed as fast as he'd climbed on and dashed into the other room.

Leah hovered in the doorway. "Why do I feel like you're trying to get rid of me?"

Isaac ducked his head for a moment and then nodded. "You're right. I want to talk about our next steps with your brother. But you don't have to worry about anything, because no matter what, I'm going to make sure you and Ben are safe."

She crossed her arms over her chest. "I know you will, but I'd still like to hear the plan."

Isaac exchanged a long look with Shane, who merely shrugged. "You might as well let her stay."

"Okay, fine. But keep in mind this isn't a democracy here. You don't get a vote on whether we go ahead with the plan or not."

She bit her lower lip and nodded. "Okay, but you have to admit that it was a good thing I was there last night, otherwise you might not have known that Lieutenant Nash was there instead of Cameron Walker."

Isaac inclined his head. "You're right about that. I just know how much you don't like hearing about the dangerous aspects of a cop's job."

"I'm over that," she said with a wave of her hand. "After everything we've been through, I think I understand what we're facing better than most."

"All right, then." Isaac stepped farther into the room and took the chair she'd used earlier. "I think we have to get in touch with Walker again," he said bluntly. "We need to set up another meeting, this time in the bright light of day."

"What if he's part of this?" Shane asked.

"We'll use a place that allows us to make sure he comes alone," Isaac said grimly. "I heard from my teammate Jenna, and she's confirmed that the gun used in the mall shooting a few weeks ago is the same one that was used to kill a gang member eighteen months ago. A gang shooting that was right in the middle of the Fifth District."

Shane grimaced. "Yeah, I've suspected that someone inside the police department is stealing guns from the evidence room and giving them to Shark and his gang to sell on the streets. For a cut of the profits, of course."

This was the first Leah had heard of it, but then again, she'd been too busy last night working with Gabriella to save Shane's life to keep up-to-date on the investigation.

"Did Cam know your theory, too?" Isaac asked.

"Yeah, and so did my boss."

Leah shivered, remembering how she'd recognized Lieutenant Nash out in the woods looking for Shane.

And she wished she knew if he was a friend or foe.

FIFTEEN

Isaac glanced curiously at Leah. She was taking all this in far better than he'd anticipated. And what exactly did "I'm over that" mean? That she'd accepted the dangers of Shane's job?

Of his job?

Or just that she'd given up trying to shield herself from the truth? He suspected the way she'd avoided talking to her brother about his job had just been a coping mechanism, especially since she worked in the trauma room. All this time, she'd known exactly what Hawk had faced. But maybe she figured it was easier to ignore the gory details if she didn't talk about them.

The real problem was that she'd already lost someone she loved and wasn't ready to open herself up to that kind of hurt again. And frankly, Isaac didn't blame her. After all, he understood exactly what she was going through. He hadn't loved Becky enough, hadn't made time to nurture his marriage, and those careless actions had cost him his son. Sure, he could blame Becky's new boyfriend, but deep down, he knew it was still his fault.

He could almost hear Leah's voice in the back of his mind, urging him to forgive himself, the way God taught them to. And he was trying.

Sitting so close to her that he could smell the cinnamon-and-spice scent that clung to her skin, he wished they had time to be alone, to talk about the growing feelings he had for her. But they didn't.

He forced himself to tear his gaze away from her and concentrate on the matter at hand. "So I'll call Cameron Walker and request a meeting. But I want a good place to meet, somewhere I can have plenty of protection and backup."

Shane grimaced and nodded. "The shed wasn't a bad place for a meeting, but I doubt he'll want to go there again."

"Maybe, maybe not." Isaac turned the idea over in his mind. Could he make it work? He was familiar with the layout, and it would be easy to see in the daylight.

Of course, daylight made it harder to hide backup, especially since it was March and the trees were still mostly bare from the lingering winter.

"Do you really think Cam Walker will agree to meet?" Leah asked doubtfully. "I still don't understand why he didn't show up last night. Why would he have sent Lieutenant Nash instead?"

"I've been thinking about that," Shane murmured. "Maybe Cam confided in the lieutenant about the proposed meeting and my boss decided to tag along. It's possible Walker was there but you didn't see him."

Isaac shook his head. "Between Leah and myself, I don't know how we could have missed him. I was inside the shed, saw the blanket you'd used and the blood from your wound. Your boss was outside, looking around the area, presumably for any sign of you. Where would Walker have been?"

Hawk shrugged and then winced and put a hand up to his injured shoulder. "Maybe he was deeper in the woods, looking for me. Did you see a vehicle of some sort?"

"No, but I didn't get a chance to do a full sweep of the area." Isaac wished he knew more, but there was no time to waste. He rubbed his hands on his jeans and stood. "I think I'll head back over to the shed now. See if I can figure out what really happened last night."

"Let me know if you find my weapon," Shane muttered.

"Wait—you can't go alone," Leah protested. "You need to take someone with you."

"I know. And I'll find someone." He hadn't

heard from Deck since the night his buddy had been called out about a suspicious package, and he'd already bothered Caleb more than enough. He should probably give Jenna a call, since she knew the most about what was going on. And at least she'd know that he needed something more than menial labor.

She answered right away when he phoned her. "Hey, I was just about to call you," she said.

"You were?" he asked in surprise. "Why? What's going on?"

"Guess who we have in custody?" she asked.

His pulse jumped. "Joey Stainwhite?"

"You got it. Griff wants you to come in, since our pal Joey had a gun on him, one with the serial numbers filed off, the same make and model as the one used at the mall shooting. You never told me exactly why you wanted me to do the ballistics match for you, and I didn't push for information. But it's clear now that whatever case you're working on has just intersected with ours."

"Good news," Isaac said, glancing toward Hawk's bedroom. He didn't want to leave Leah, Ben and Hawk here alone, but at the same time, he hated to call Caleb back again after he'd just left. "I'll come in to talk to Stainwhite, but I need someone to come out here to keep my friend's sister and her son safe."

"Maybe give Declan a call?" she suggested.

"I can try. Tell Griff I'll be there soon." Isaac disconnected, thrilled to know that they finally had a break in the case.

He quickly dialed Deck's phone and was frustrated when his buddy didn't answer. There must be something going on, since Isaac hadn't heard from him in a few days, but he left a terse message asking for a return call anyway. Then he turned and headed back toward Hawk's bedroom.

Maybe if he gave his buddy his weapon to use, he could protect Leah and Ben for the short time Isaac was gone. Hawk was right-handed and the injury was to his left shoulder. And it wasn't as if anyone knew they were even here. This cabin had proved to be safe over the past twenty-four hours, so staying here awhile longer shouldn't matter.

Besides, grilling Joey Stainwhite wouldn't take too long. Isaac could be there and back in a couple of hours.

He went in and proposed his plan. Leah didn't look thrilled at the idea of his going in to talk to Joey Stainwhite, but she didn't protest.

Hawk gladly took the gun and Isaac understood that his buddy no doubt felt unsettled without his own weapon, which he'd lost somewhere outside the shed. "Don't worry. We'll be fine. Just see if you can get that guy to spill his guts, okay?"

"I'll do my best," Isaac promised.

Leah smiled weakly as she followed him out of Hawk's room. "I know it's silly, but be safe, okay?"

"I'm going to our headquarters," he reminded her. "There's nothing unsafe about it."

"I know that logically." She tapped her temple. "But I can't seem to shake the bad feeling in my gut."

"Oh, Leah," he said with a sigh. He reached out, pulled her into his arms and was glad when she wrapped hers tightly around his waist. "I promise you, I'll always be careful. I have too much to live for." It hadn't always been true. In those early days following Jeremy's death, Isaac had been a little too reckless, figuring nothing could hurt him as much as losing his son.

But now Leah, Ben and even Hawk were counting on him.

And he'd discovered that life was very much worth living.

"I'll pray for you," Leah said, her voice muffled against his shirt.

"I appreciate that," he said and meant it. "I've learned a lot about faith since meeting you, but I'm sure there's more to know."

Leah tipped her head back and gazed up at him. "I'd like to teach you once this is all over," she said.

"I'll take you up on that offer." He lowered his

head and kissed her, hoping to show her with actions rather than words how he felt.

"Mommy, are you kissing Mr. Isaac?" Ben asked.

Leah quickly broke off the kiss, color flagging her cheeks. "Um, yes. He's leaving, so I'm kissing him goodbye."

Isaac coughed to hide a laugh. "That's right," he said, striving for a serious tone.

Ben looked perplexed. "But that's not the way you kiss Uncle Shane," he said with childlike logic.

Isaac glanced at Leah, who was studiously ignoring him. "Yes, well, that's because Isaac and I are friends and Uncle Shane is family. I think you should draw your uncle Shane a picture," she said, changing the subject. "Just like you did for Mr. Isaac."

"Okay." Leah's diversion worked and Ben ran over to get his paper and crayons.

Leah still looked embarrassed and Isaac decided not to push the issue, since he needed to leave. "I'll be back soon," he promised.

"I know." She smiled and then turned to follow her son. It was difficult to let her go without another kiss.

But they'd have time later to talk. Right now, it was time to get to work.

* * *

The drive back to Milwaukee seemed to take forever, but it was only twenty-five minutes later when he pulled into the lot and parked his borrowed vehicle next to the police-issued ones.

Griff and Jenna were waiting for him when he strode inside.

"You better fill me in on what's going on," Griff said with a scowl.

"I know." Isaac quickly described how Hawk's undercover stint had gone bad and how he'd been shot. "I can give you more details later, but right now I need to know where Stainwhite was picked up," he said to Griff.

His boss nodded and shrugged. "Actually, we got lucky. Someone called in an anonymous tip saying that Stainwhite would be at Stan's Liquor Store, so we sent a couple of deputies, and sure enough, there he was."

"A tip, huh?" Seemed odd that they'd get a call like that, although sometimes districts offered minor rewards for information, so maybe someone was desperate for a little cash. "Okay, let's see what he has to say."

"He's in room 1 with his public defender. Take Reed with you."

"Sure thing." Protocol was always to have two deputies present during an interview, so he followed Jenna as they headed over to where Stain-white and his lawyer were waiting.

"Hey, Steel, how's it going?" Isaac said cheerfully.

Joey's scowl deepened. "Only my friends call me Steel," he said.

"Yeah, well, my friends call me Ice. Maybe you remember me better by that name."

Recognition dawned in Joey's sunken eyes. "You're a cop now?" he asked incredulously.

"Yep, and I'm the guy who's going to put you behind bars for attempted murder of a police officer."

"No way will you be able to claim attempted murder," the attorney declared.

"Yeah, I never tried to shoot no cop," Joey protested. "You got the wrong guy."

"See, that's where you're wrong, Steel. Because I saw you inside Stan's Liquor Store and watched you exchange a gun for a thick wad of cash. You saw me, came outside and stood in the middle of the road, firing directly at me in my car. I'm thinking the slug I pulled out of the seat is going to match that gun you had on you when you were arrested. I've got you cold, Steel. Who do you think the jury is going to believe? Me, a trusted cop, or a loser like you?"

All Joey's bravado vanished as he realized there

was no chance to escape the charges. The lawyer didn't look too happy, either.

"Maybe we can do something for you," Jenna said, leaning forward to brace her elbows on the table. "But we'll need you to cooperate with us. Maybe tell us who all is involved in your little gun scheme?"

"Will you take attempted murder of a police officer off the table if he does?" the attorney asked.

"No way. I'm not going to snitch for you," Joey said abruptly, ignoring his lawyer. "He'll kill me if I do."

"Who will kill you? Shark?" Isaac pressed.

There was a flicker of recognition in Joey's eyes a moment before he shook his head. "Don't know anyone by that name," he said, crossing his arms. "You may as well take me back to my cell, 'cause I'm not talking."

Isaac exchanged a knowing glance with Jenna as Stainwhite's attorney tried to talk some sense into his client.

But in the end, they didn't get anything from him.

"I really thought he'd talk," Jenna said with a heavy sigh.

"I know. I thought so, too." Isaac glanced at his watch. "I gotta get back to Leah and Ben, but let me know if the ballistics match the slug I pulled out of my car, okay?"

"Will do," his teammate agreed.

Isaac strode outside to his car, anxious to get back to the log cabin. He hadn't gotten much from Stainwhite, but at least he knew the guy was off the streets for a while.

And there was always the chance that Steel might change his mind about spilling his guts after spending a few days behind bars.

Leah couldn't believe she'd allowed herself to get carried away in Isaac's kiss. She was mortified that Ben had caught them. Her son had never seen her with a man other than his father.

Never seen her with a man, period.

She told herself to get a grip, that there was no reason to believe she'd scarred Ben for life or anything.

But she did worry about her son getting too attached to Isaac. Maybe now that Shane was here, Ben wouldn't vie for Isaac's attention as much.

"Leah? Do you have a minute?" her brother called.

She hurried over. "Sure. What's up?"

"My phone battery is dead. Do you think you could charge it up with your adapters?"

"If it fits," she said, taking his cell and peering at the connection. "You're in luck. Looks to be the same kind that Isaac bought."

She went into the kitchen to get the charger,

then took it to Shane's room. She plugged in the phone and handed it back to him. "You're not thinking of contacting that ATF guy, are you?"

"Yeah, I am." Shane stared at the cell for a minute. "I feel like I need to do something. We can't just sit here and wait for something to happen."

"Wait until Isaac gets here," she suggested. "Maybe he'll know something more that will help."

"All right," Shane conceded. "But the more I think about it, the more I believe you guys missed seeing Cameron Walker last night. He must have been there."

Leah lifted her hands helplessly. "He could have been," she agreed. "But I panicked when I saw your boss."

"Understandable." Shane yawned and blinked. "I don't know why I'm so tired."

"Your body is fighting off that nasty infection," she murmured drily. "Take a nap. Your next dose isn't due for another couple of hours."

Shane pried his eyelids open. "Not until Isaac returns."

At that moment she heard the sound of a car engine. "I think he might be back," she said.

"Stay here," Shane commanded as he swung his legs over the side of the bed. "I'll check it out to make sure it's him."

Leah refrained from rolling her eyes, considering he'd just leaned heavily on her when he'd gotten up to use the bathroom. "Don't be silly—stay here. I'll peek through the window to make sure."

Without waiting for him to respond, she walked over and parted the curtains with her fingertip, relieved to see Isaac driving the old familiar sedan up to the cabin.

He hadn't been gone all that long, but the place had seemed empty without him.

Or maybe she'd just missed having him around.

"Don't worry. It's Isaac," she said to Shane.

"Good. I hope he managed to get some new information."

Isaac came in a few minutes later and headed straight for Shane's room. "Hey, how's it going?" he asked.

"You tell me," Leah's brother countered. "Tell me you got something to go on."

"Unfortunately, I didn't," he responded. "Steel wouldn't talk, despite his lawyer trying his best to convince him. He's scared to death of Shark."

"Figures," Shane muttered. "So now what?"

"I guess that's up to you," Isaac said. "Do you think we can trust Cam Walker and your boss?"

"Can't Griff help us?" Leah spoke up. "You said yourself that Shane's case is intertwined with yours now."

"Different jurisdictions," her brother said with a grimace. "I'm not sure how well that will go over."

"Griff has to be careful not to step on the Milwaukee P.D.'s toes," Isaac said. "But he might be willing to offer some help."

"I would hope so," she said with exasperation.

"Mommy, there's a man outside," Ben said from the other room.

"What?" Her heart leaped into her throat and she rushed over to where her son was sitting on the bed surrounded by his toy cars. "Are you sure?" she whispered.

Ben nodded. "I was looking for the deers but saw a man instead."

"I'm going to head outside to take a look," Isaac said. "Get Ben and take him into Shane's room."

She didn't need to be told twice. She scooped her son into her arms, allowing him to grab a couple of his toy cars to bring along, before following Isaac into the other room.

"I need my gun, just in case," Isaac said, reaching over Shane's lap for the weapon. "Stay down until I call all clear."

"Will do."

Leah swallowed hard and held Ben close. In the time they'd been here, they hadn't seen any other occupants, but surely they weren't the only ones around. It was highly likely that Ben had seen someone harmless, since it was broad daylight.

She desperately wanted to believe that the man

Ben had seen didn't intend to harm them, but deep down, she feared the worst.

That whoever had shot Shane had managed to find them.

SIXTEEN

Isaac moved silently through the wooded area around their cabin, his weapon held down at his side. Maybe he was overreacting to what Ben had seen, but he'd feel better once he knew for sure who was out there.

At first he didn't see anyone at all, but then he caught a glimpse of a man wearing a knit cap, standing behind a tree. Isaac's gut tightened in warning. Anyone innocent wouldn't be hiding like that.

Whoever this guy might be, he was clearly up to no good.

Isaac stayed in the shadows, moving so that he could get a better angle to see the man's face. He debated going back inside the cabin, but at that moment the guy moved out from behind the tree. He crouched low and ran across to a different set of trees, farther away.

Isaac frowned when he realized the man had

gone to an area directly across from their cabin. From this new position he could watch the doorway.

A slow burn of anger had Isaac gripping his weapon tightly. He needed to take this guy out of the picture, but he would have to take a wide route in order to come up from behind and catch him unaware.

Hopefully, he'd be too busy watching the cabin to realize Isaac was behind him.

He hoped and prayed Leah and Ben would stay hidden beside Shane and keep away from the front door.

Moving slowly, Isaac melted into the trees and made his way round to get behind him. The trek took longer than he'd anticipated, and he still couldn't get a clear glimpse of the man's face.

When he finally had the guy in his line of vision, just a few feet ahead, he stealthily crept up behind him.

Isaac let out a soundless breath and then made his move, jumping forward and shoving against the man's back so that he was pinned against the tree. He pressed his gun against the guy's temple. "Don't move or I'll shoot. Drop your weapon— slow and easy so I don't flinch and accidentally kill you."

The man's body went tense, but he did as Isaac commanded, holding his gun out from his right side and dropping it to the ground. "Listen, my name is Lieutenant Nash and I'm with the Fifth District Police," he said. "You don't know what you're in the middle of, but you need to let me go so I can do my job. Innocent lives are at stake."

"Yeah, I'm well aware of the illegal gunrunning scam that is being partially funded with confiscated weapons from your precinct," Isaac said in a low tone. "And I don't trust you, so put your hands behind your head."

"You're making a big mistake," Lieutenant Nash said as he once again complied with Isaac's directive. "I'm not the leak inside the department. Trey Birchwood was the one leaking information. You have the wrong man."

"Maybe, maybe not, but we're not going to have this conversation right here." Isaac frantically considered what he could use to tie him up with, since he hadn't thought to bring rope or duct tape. He tugged on the string from his sweatshirt hood, thinking it was better than nothing.

And he'd have to trust that Nash didn't have a death wish and wouldn't try to run.

Just then Isaac noticed another man approaching the cabin from the other direction, wearing an ATF jacket. Cameron Walker? Most likely.

He took Nash's right wrist and twisted his arm behind his back, holding the gun at his side. He needed two hands to tie him up and didn't want to drop his weapon even for a second.

"Hey, good work," the ATF agent said as Isaac prodded Nash to walk toward the clearing. "You caught our dirty cop."

Isaac nodded, unable to deny that it certainly seemed that way. "Hold a gun on him while I tie him up," he said to Walker. "Nash, get down on the ground with your hands behind your back."

The lieutenant did as he was told, dropping to his knees and putting his arms behind his back. Isaac slipped his gun in the waistband of his jeans and wrapped the sweatshirt string tightly around Nash's wrists. But instead of helping him, Cam Walker dashed toward the cabin, kicked the door open and darted inside.

"What in the world?" Isaac quickly finished tying the knot and then let go of Nash, leaping to his feet. In that second he realized he'd made a grave mistake.

Walker had to be the guy who'd blown Hawk's cover, not Nash. Isaac had trusted the wrong guy!

He followed Cameron Walker inside and then froze when he realized Walker was already in Hawk's room, holding a gun on Leah, who was clutching Ben. For a moment Isaac couldn't breathe, flashing back to when Becky's new boyfriend had held a gun on Jeremy mere seconds before he'd pulled the trigger.

Please, Lord, please spare Leah and Ben!

"Stay where you are and drop the gun," Walker said harshly. "I have nothing to lose and I plan to kill you all anyway, so it doesn't matter to me if the woman and kid go first."

The last thing Isaac wanted to do was drop his weapon, but he slowly did as he'd been ordered, crouching as he did so.

"Kick it toward me," Walker commanded.

He kicked it under Hawk's bed instead so that it couldn't be used against them. Leah cried out in pain as Walker yanked her head back by her hair and pressed the gun more firmly against her temple. Ben started crying and Isaac could tell that the sound was bugging the gunman. The way the guy shifted his stance and glared at Ben reminded him of that first night, when a gunman had held Leah hostage.

Isaac believed this had to be the same man who'd tried to kidnap Leah and Ben and killed Trey Birchwood.

But why had he killed Trey? That didn't make any sense, based on what Nash had told him.

"You do anything like that again and I'll blow her away," Walker said in a furious tone. "Understand?"

Isaac swallowed hard, feeling sick to his stomach, and nodded. He needed to remember every bit of his hostage-negotiator training. "Understood. Tell you what, Walker—let the woman and the boy go and I'll be your hostage instead."

"No way," Walker said with a leering grin. "In fact, you're going to help me set this crime scene up to look like you did it."

The sick feeling in his gut intensified. There had to be a way to get through to this guy, but how?

"You're not the real Cam Walker, are you?" Hawk said from his perch on the bed. Isaac noticed now that Shane was sitting upright on the edge, directly across from where Walker held Leah and Ben.

"Sure I am," the ATF agent said.

"No, I can tell your voice is different," Hawk said with certainty. "I spoke to the real Cameron Walker many times and I know you're not him. So who are you? I bet you killed Walker and stole his identity."

"So what?" the impostor said offhandedly. "You'll never know who I really am, so don't even bother asking."

"How did you find us?" Isaac asked. He knew he had to find a way to keep the fake ATF agent talking and hoped stroking his ego might work. All he needed was enough time for Nash to get free. Since he'd rushed at the end, he figured the lieutenant just might be able to work his way loose from the sweatshirt string and come in to help them. Or at least call for backup.

Unless he really was working with the fake Walker?

No, somehow it didn't seem like it. But even if so, there was nothing Isaac could do about it right now.

"Let me guess," he continued when the ATF agent didn't say anything. "You had someone call in the anonymous tip about Steel and then somehow tracked my car here, right?"

"Yeah, that's right," the ATF impostor sneered. "I knew your cop buddy was getting help from someone within the sheriff's department, and when you put the APB out on Stainwhite, I figured you were the key. It was pathetically easy to put a tracking device on your car and to follow you here."

Isaac wanted to kick himself for not figuring it out sooner, but it was no use worrying about that now. "And how does Nash fit in?" he asked.

A momentary flash of confusion washed over the guy's face and Isaac knew that the fake ATF agent didn't have a clue as to who was tied up outside. What did that mean? That the cop really was trying to help them?

"Where's Sharkey?" Hawk asked, changing the subject. "I'm surprised he's not here with you."

"He's not the leader of this arrangement," the

fake Walker said smoothly. "And enough talking. We're going to set this up so that Hawkins takes the fall."

Isaac could barely stand to see the look of fear etched on Leah's face, and Ben's sobs tore at his heart. He racked his brain for another way to stall. And where was Nash? Shouldn't he have figured out a way to get free of his bonds by now?

"Looks like the sheriff's deputy has to be the first one to die," the fake ATF agent mused. "And then the woman and the kid, with the undercover cop the last, by his own hand, of course."

Isaac glanced at Hawk and saw his muscles tense. In that moment he understood what his buddy intended to do.

Without any other warning, Hawk launched himself at the impostor, who reacted by swinging the gun away from Leah toward the new threat. Hawk hit his arm a split second before the gun went off, sending a bullet whistling above his head. Isaac dived toward the fake agent as well, while Leah and Ben scrambled out of the way. From the corner of his eye, Isaac noted that she pushed her son into the farthest corner of the room, placing herself directly in front of him.

Isaac admired her courage. In fact, he admired a lot about her, and hopefully, he would have time to tell her.

With Hawk's help, he managed to get the Walker

impostor subdued. Isaac held the man's hands behind his back, while Hawk tied him up with a string he tore off the miniblinds.

Nash finally barreled into the cabin, holding his gun, which he must have gone back to find in the woods, where Isaac had made him drop it. Nash crossed over, glaring at the impostor.

"Aaron Winslow, you're under arrest for murder, selling illegal guns and anything else we can pin on you," Lieutenant Nash said harshly.

Isaac sighed, relieved to know it was finally over. He glanced over at Leah and Ben, wanting nothing more than to get them out of here.

"Look out!" Hawk shouted.

Isaac whirled around, horrified to see that Nash was aiming his weapon at him, rather than at Winslow. What was going on? Was Nash involved after all? Had he only pretended to arrest Winslow to gain access to the cabin?

Ben broke away from Leah and ran directly toward him, so he launched himself in front of the boy as two gunshots echoed through the cabin.

A deep, fiery pain slashed at his left side and he dropped to his knees, desperately glancing around to make sure that Ben was all right. The little boy was sobbing as Leah held him, but thankfully, there was no sign of blood. Isaac caught a glimpse of Shane holding Walker's gun toward Nash before darkness claimed him.

His last conscious thought was to thank God that Leah and Ben were finally safe.

"Leah, are you and Ben all right?" Shane asked, stumbling toward her.

"Y-yes," she managed to gasp, her mind still reeling from the events. Lieutenant Nash was lying on the floor, his chest soaked with blood where her brother had shot him. She forced herself to cross over to be sure he was dead before turning her attention to Isaac.

"Call 911," she told Shane. She grabbed the IV supplies and what was left of the gauze dressings from the bedside table and knelt beside Isaac.

Her heart squeezed when she saw the amount of blood soaking through his sweatshirt. She lifted the hem and pushed the fabric out of the way in order to assess the extent of the damage.

There was an entry wound that didn't look too terrible, but she felt along the back for the exit wound, knowing from experience that it would be far worse. The only good news was that the wound was on the edge of his side and the bullet wasn't still inside his body.

Her fingers shook as she opened gauze and pressed it over the front wound. Taking care of someone she knew and cared for was very different from treating strangers in the E.R. But she forced herself to think and act like a nurse.

"Shane, I need your help. We have to roll him over and hold pressure on the exit wound."

Her brother was holding Ben with his good arm, but came over and set his nephew down on the floor. "All right, easy now." Together they managed to shift Isaac's weight so that he was lying on his right side. Maintaining pressure wouldn't be easy to accomplish from this angle, but it was worth a shot.

"Here, hold this," she said, putting a larger pad of gauze over the exit wound.

"Mommy, I'm scared," Ben said, trying to crawl into her lap. She wanted to hug and hold her son, but she needed to keep working to keep Isaac alive.

"Come on, Ben—why don't you come over here," Shane said. He tucked Ben close while still pressing on Isaac's wound.

"Okay," the boy said, sniffling loudly. He stayed close and then reached over to put his small hands on top of Shane's as if he wanted to help. She was worried about how Ben was handling all this, but at least he'd stopped crying.

"I love you, Ben," she said with a reassuring smile. She rolled up Isaac's sleeve to start an IV. His veins hadn't totally collapsed, which was a good sign that he hadn't lost too much blood.

Leah quickly inserted an IV in Isaac's forearm

and hung a bag of fluids. She had only one left, so she hoped the ambulance would get here soon.

"How did you know Nash was involved?" she asked as she regulated the IV fluids. She'd never been so scared as when she'd watched Isaac leap in front of Ben.

He'd risked his life to save her son's.

"Winslow was from District Three, so the only way Nash could have known Winslow was involved was if he was in on it, too." Shane lifted his gaze to hers. "Trey told me he thought he saw Winslow and Nash together, but I wasn't sure if I could believe him. Now I wish I had, because I'm pretty sure Trey died as a result of seeing them together."

Leah closed her eyes for a moment, wishing that so many people hadn't had to die before they'd discovered the truth. She had a better appreciation for why Shane and Isaac chose to work in law enforcement. Criminals shouldn't be allowed to get away with murder.

"Will Mr. Isaac wake up?" Ben asked, his lower lip quivering.

"I'm certain he will," she assured him, even though she couldn't tell how much damage had been done internally. With the wound so close to the edge, he had a good chance. She leaned forward and smoothed her hand down the side of his face. "Isaac, can you hear me? You're going to be okay. Just hang on for the ambulance to arrive. Please, hang on."

"We should pray for him," Ben suggested.

A lump filled her throat, but she nodded. "Yes," she croaked. "We should."

"God, please make Mr. Isaac better," Ben said.

"Amen," Leah murmured, tears swimming in her eyes.

"Amen," Shane echoed. She noticed he kept glancing over to make sure the Walker impersonator was still trussed up.

A thumping noise caught her attention and she lifted her head in alarm. "Shane, do you hear that?"

"Take over here and I'll check it out," he said, rising to his feet.

She pressed on Isaac's injuries, using as much strength as she could, while hoping and praying that the sound wasn't an indication of more bad news.

But as the noise grew louder she recognized it as a helicopter. Could it be the Flight For Life aircraft coming for Isaac?

Shane poked his head through the bedroom door. "Help is here," he announced. "Police and the hospital chopper. Too many trees to land here, so they're putting it down on the road and will carry him out via stretcher."

"Thank goodness," Leah murmured.

Shane crossed over to where the fake Walker was lying facedown on the floor. "The cops have a lot of questions for you," he said, dragging him to his feet. He pressed the gun against his side and marched him past Leah, Ben and Isaac. "Starting with what happened to Cameron Walker."

Leah watched them leave, feeling a little sorry for the man who'd chosen the wrong path.

"Where's the injured cop?" someone shouted from the doorway.

"In here," Leah called. She forced herself to back away as two paramedics hurried into the room. "He has a through-and-through gunshot wound on the left side, and I've hung a liter of fluid and put on a pressure dressing."

"Nice. You've made our job that much easier," the first paramedic said in an admiring tone. "We're going to get him hooked up to our portable monitor and then transport him to the chopper."

"Are you taking him to Trinity Medical Center?" she asked. She wasn't sure which level-one trauma center was closest and hoped Isaac would be taken to the hospital she worked at.

"Yep. You can meet us there," he told her.

Nodding in agreement, she pulled Ben close as the paramedics made quick work of getting Isaac on the stretcher and wheeling him out of the cabin.

"Did you hear that, Ben? Our prayers have been answered."

"I'm glad, Mommy."

"Me, too," she whispered.

Now she needed to make sure that Isaac pulled through without any problem.

Because suddenly, she couldn't imagine her life without him.

SEVENTEEN

Isaac awoke to a throbbing pain along his left side, a fuzzy head and a serious case of cotton mouth. He squinted in the bright sunlight streaming through the window, trying to figure out where he was. The sight of an IV pump next to the bed reminded him of Hawk.

And Leah.

Concern pushed him further awake and he glanced around, noticing with a frown that he was in a hospital room. Alone. Where was everyone? There was a cup of water on a table beside him, so he reached out and took a tentative sip.

So far, so good. Now if only he could find someone with a few answers.

As if on cue, a tall man wearing a white lab coat entered the room, accompanied by a young woman wearing scrubs.

"Good morning, Mr. Morrison," the man said in greeting. "I'm Dr. Lansing, the surgeon who patched you up yesterday afternoon."

Yesterday afternoon? Alarm shot through him. "I've been out for twenty-four hours?"

"Well, technically, a little over sixteen, since you didn't get out of surgery until after 5:00 p.m. last night, and it's about 9:15 in the morning," the woman said with a smile. "I'm Claire, your nurse for the day."

Sixteen hours still sounded far too long, but right now he needed answers. "Okay, Doc, how bad is it?" Isaac asked, preferring to know the true extent of his injuries.

"Not as bad as I expected," Dr. Lansing admitted. "The trauma nurse who cared for you on the scene pretty much saved your life. By the time you arrived here you were relatively stable, and other than a spleen laceration and some muscle damage, you're doing great. You'll need to take it easy for a while, though, so that you don't cause that laceration to start bleeding again."

Leah had saved his life. He'd spent days trying to protect her and Ben, but in the end, she'd saved him.

He owed her a huge debt of gratitude.

"How long will I need to be off duty?" he asked, sensing the doc wasn't going to stick around for long.

"He's a sheriff's deputy," Claire interjected helpfully.

"Ten to twelve weeks," Dr. Lansing said.

"Although I'm sure they can assign you some desk work after the first six weeks or so. Now, let's take a look at your wounds."

He grimaced and nodded. "Sure."

Claire helped him turn onto his right side so that they could look at his front and back wounds. While they changed his dressing, he gritted his teeth against the pain, not willing to complain and risk fuzzy-head syndrome from taking narcotics. He wondered if he should call his boss or wait for Griff to come to him.

"Everything looks good," Dr. Lansing pronounced, stripping off his gloves and heading over to the sink to wash his hands. The nurse finished taping his dressings in place before doing the same.

"Thanks for everything," Isaac said. Despite Leah's concerns about police work being a dangerous job, he'd actually never been shot in the line of duty before. Minor injuries, sure, but never anything serious.

Nothing requiring surgery.

Truth be told, he'd had more injuries when he'd run wild on the streets, before being sent to Saint Jermaine's.

"No problem. We're going to watch you for one more day before springing you out of here," Dr. Lansing added. "You'll need IV antibiotics for twenty-four hours, and we like to make sure your lab work remains stable before sending you home."

"Sounds good."

"You're lucky that bullet wasn't a half inch to the right," the doc added as the nurse made several notations in a computer system located in the corner of his room. "You would have lost several inches of your large intestine and possibly your left kidney."

"I understand. Thanks again." The close call wasn't lost on him. Isaac suspected Leah would say that God was watching over him, and after everything that had happened, he'd agree.

But where was she now? Had Hawk taken Leah and Ben home?

The fact that they weren't here seemed to send a glaring message. Not that he could really blame her, considering how close she'd come to losing her son. That moment Ben had rushed out in the line of fire was deeply etched in Isaac's mind. Which made him wonder if Leah had decided to move on with putting her life back together.

Without him.

Leah was glad to be able to sleep in her own bed. She knew Ben was also glad to be home, although that didn't stop him from having nightmares. After getting up twice to see to him, she'd let Ben crawl in with her. Thankfully, they'd both slept better after that.

Now that she was up, though, she desperately wanted to get back to the hospital to see how Isaac was doing.

Last evening, she'd told Isaac's boss, Griff Vaughn, everything she knew about what had happened, even as she worried about how Isaac was doing in surgery. Thankfully, the nursing staff knew her very well and popped out to give her updates.

Griff had spoken extensively with Shane, as well. From what she'd overheard, it sounded as if they'd used fingerprints to prove that the man who'd pretended to be Cameron Walker was in fact Aaron Winslow, as Lieutenant Nash had said. And thankfully, Winslow had agreed to cooperate for the chance of a lighter sentence. He had provided details on the illegal gun deals, admitting to taking weapons from the evidence room. Shane had seemed shocked to discover that a couple of districts were involved, which meant a huge Internal Affairs investigation was under way. And of course, they put out a warrant for Wade Sharkey's arrest.

It was hard to believe the danger was finally over. Or at least it would be once Ben stopped having nightmares and things got back into a normal routine. Leah had spoken with her own boss and explained everything. Her boss had been sympathetic and had given Leah the rest of the week off.

Since Ben was still sleeping, she decided to take a quick shower. Wearing clean clothes was a nice change, even though she debated far too long about which sweater to wear, as if Isaac would even notice. She shook her head at her own idiocy.

After she'd finished changing her clothes for the last time, Ben woke up and rubbed his eyes sleepily. "Mom, can we have pancakes for breakfast?"

"Um, sure." She was anxious to get to the hospital, but cooking pancakes wouldn't take that long. Truthfully, she should have gotten Ben up to go to school, but after his rough night, she'd figured it would be better to keep him home one more day. He was a bright kid and would be able to catch up quickly from the few days he'd missed.

Besides, she knew he needed to see for himself that Isaac was okay. Several times during his nightmares he'd cried out Isaac's name. She knew what he was going through, since the same image of Isaac leaping in front of Ben played over and over in her mind, too.

Isaac had risked his life for her son and she owed him more than she could ever repay.

Ben seemed to cheer up after finishing his

favorite breakfast. She hoped that once he saw Isaac was okay, he'd get over having bad dreams.

Leah hadn't let herself think beyond making sure Isaac was doing all right, but as she drove to the hospital, too many questions began to filter through her mind.

Would he want to see her again once he was released from the hospital? Or would they both go their separate ways? Did Ben remind him too much of his young son, Jeremy? Or was he ready to move on?

Was she ready to move on?

She tried to push away the never-ending thoughts ruminating in her head, but it wasn't easy. She felt more confused now than she had before. Being back home, thinking about the mundane aspects of her life, she couldn't imagine what she and Isaac even had in common.

No doubt she was making a big deal out of nothing. Isaac had never so much as hinted at a future between them. She was reading far too much into a simple kiss.

Well, a not-so-simple kiss.

She parked in the employee structure and walked inside with Ben. She knew where Isaac's room was located, as she'd stayed with him for a couple of hours after surgery. She'd wanted to remain until he'd woken up, but Ben had yawned so widely his jaw had popped, and she'd realized she needed to get home for her son's sake.

Shane hadn't gone home. He'd been admitted to a hospital room on the same floor as Isaac, just as a safety measure to make sure he was recovering well enough from his own gunshot wound.

Leah debated whom to visit first and told herself that Ben's need to make sure Isaac was okay was more important than seeing her brother.

Even if she knew deep down that her need to see Isaac was more important, too.

As she approached his room, her steps slowed when she heard voices coming from the partially open doorway. At first she thought maybe the doctor was in there, but soon realized that wasn't the case.

"I can't believe you didn't bring me into this from the very beginning," a deep voice that sounded like Griff Vaughn's said. "And that you risked your life while not being officially on the job."

"I'm not going to apologize for risking my life for a child," Isaac said sternly. "I understand you're upset, and I'm sorry I didn't include you earlier. But I didn't have a speck of proof and it was my responsibility to keep Leah and Ben safe."

"Your responsibility is to me and the rest of your

team," Griff responded harshly. "And you need to know the sheriff isn't at all happy about this."

Leah stepped away from Isaac's doorway, going down the hall until she couldn't hear them speaking. She shouldn't have been eavesdropping in the first place, but she'd been curious as to what Dr. Lansing had to say.

Unfortunately, she'd heard too much. The idea that Isaac might lose his job over her made her feel sick to her stomach. Ironic, since at one time she'd wished for exactly that.

"Mommy, where's Mr. Isaac?" Ben asked.

She glanced down at him. "Um, I think he's busy right now. Maybe we'll go visit Uncle Shane first, okay?"

Before she finished speaking, Griff Vaughn strode out of Isaac's room, his face darker than a thundercloud. His gaze locked on hers for a long heartbeat before he gave her a brief nod and strode toward the elevator.

This probably wasn't a good time to visit Isaac.

But Ben's lower lip trembled and she remembered his nightmares. "But I wanna see Mr. Isaac," he protested. "You said we could. You said he was better!"

She sighed and gave in. "Okay, but we can't stay too long," she cautioned, hoping that Isaac wouldn't mind.

They approached the doorway and she gave a tentative knock.

A deep raspy voice called, "Come in."

She pushed the door open and stepped over the threshold, holding Ben's hand. "Hi, how are you doing?"

A tired smile bloomed on Isaac's face. "Good. Better, now that you're here."

"Mr. Isaac," Ben cried, rushing over to the bed. "You're awake!"

Isaac's curious gaze met Leah's, but he addressed her son. "Yep, I'm awake. No need to worry. I'm doing great."

"We prayed and prayed for you," Ben said solemnly.

"Thank you, Ben," Isaac murmured. "I prayed for you and your mom, too. I was hoping you were both doing all right."

"I had bad dreams," the little boy said. He clasped the side rail and tried to climb up onto the bed.

"Whoa, there, what are you doing?" Leah rushed over to lift her son away. "You'll make Mr. Isaac's wound worse if you climb in with him."

"Nah, I'll be fine," Isaac protested.

She threw him an exasperated glance. "Don't be silly. What did the doctor have to say?"

Isaac shrugged. "Something about a laceration in my spleen and muscle damage. I'm off work for at least six to eight weeks, and then I can have desk duty."

She wasn't surprised and had a hunch that desk duty wasn't high on Isaac's list of fun things to do. "I need to thank you for saving Ben's life," she said in a low tone.

But he was already shaking his head. "According to the doc, you saved my life, too, so I think we're even."

She knew that wasn't true. He wouldn't have died from a lack of IV tubing, although maybe putting pressure on his wounds had helped. She longed to cross over and give him a hug, but couldn't seem to force herself to move from the spot.

"Well, we're glad to see you're doing fine," she said with forced cheerfulness. "We have to head over to see Shane, too. I don't know if you realize that they kept him here overnight."

Isaac scowled and struggled to push himself upright. "I didn't know. But hang on—I want to go with you."

"Don't you think you should wait for your nurse?"

"She told me I should get up and walk, so that's what I'm going to do." Isaac tugged a robe over his hospital gown and then swung his legs over the side of the bed. He swayed precariously and Leah went to steady him.

"Hang on. We need to make sure you don't pull out that IV." She waited a moment for him to get his bearings before leaving his side to head over to the other side of the room. After unplugging the IV pole, she wheeled it around the bed so that they could take it with them.

"Ready?" she asked.

Isaac gave a determined nod and stood. He grimaced and grasped the pole for support.

"Do you want something for pain?" she asked.

"Nope," he replied. "Where is your brother's room?"

"At the other end of the hall. This is the trauma-surgery floor. Most trauma postoperative patients come here."

"Handy," Isaac muttered as he moved awkwardly behind the IV pole.

"Isn't it, though," she agreed, keeping a sharp eye on him in case he stumbled and fell.

Ben skipped along beside them, clearly happy after seeing Isaac. Shane's room was at the very end of the corridor, farthest from the nurses' station and near the stairwell leading down to the lobby level.

"I'll get the door," Leah said, going around Isaac to push Shane's door open. She held Ben back, giving Isaac plenty of room to maneuver his way inside.

But when she followed Isaac into her brother's

room, she stopped abruptly when she realized Shane wasn't alone.

Wade Sharkey was standing there, holding a gun. And when he flashed his evil smile, she swallowed a wave of nausea and pushed Ben behind her.

It was broad daylight, in a busy hospital, but apparently the danger wasn't over.

And somehow, she got the sense that Sharkey didn't care about his own life as much as he cared about seeking revenge.

Isaac couldn't believe that he'd brought Leah and Ben into the line of fire once again.

Why hadn't he considered Sharkey brazen enough to come into the hospital to finish them off? And Isaac was standing there in a hospital gown without a weapon in sight.

"Close the door," Sharkey said harshly.

Leah was closest to it and Isaac wished she'd make a run for it, but of course she didn't. Instead she reached out and pushed the door shut behind her.

"Well, well, if it isn't Hawk's pretty sister and Ice." Sharkey's gun didn't waver one inch. "This is perfect. I can take you all out at once."

"And risk getting arrested?" Hawk drawled. "I don't think so."

Sharkey laughed, the evil sound sending a

chill down Isaac's spine. He knew full well what Shark was capable of. What he didn't know was if the guy was unbalanced enough to give up his own life for his cause. "You think I'm afraid of a couple of hospital security guards? They're not armed. I'll be out of here and down the staircase before anyone can catch me."

The certainty in Sharkey's voice worried him. Had he cased out the hospital somehow, finding the perfect escape route? The guy was clearly a cold-blooded killer and would stop at nothing to make sure his tracks were covered.

Isaac tried to think past the pain. There had to be a way out of this mess. His gaze landed on the bedside table, and he remembered how Leah had used it to help bring down a meth addict.

Maybe he could do something similar. He didn't have a gun, but he had an IV pole.

And there was no time to waste.

"There are cops downstairs right now," Hawk said flatly. "My captain told me he'd be here by eleven o'clock and it's two minutes to. You'd better get out while you can."

The attempt at a diversion worked. The minute Sharkey glanced up at the clock, Isaac made his move, shoving the bedside table into him as hard as he could and then grabbing the IV pole and swinging it at Sharkey's head.

Leah screamed from behind him and he hoped

she and Ben were making a run for it. Hawk leaped out of the bed and somehow managed to grab Sharkey's gun.

Isaac managed to get Shark on the floor and held the IV pole across his upper chest, pressing down with every ounce of strength he possessed. He felt the sutures in his side pop open and warm fluid gush down his side, but he ignored it.

"You can let him up now," Hawk said, holding the gun steady.

"Not until help arrives," Isaac muttered. After yesterday's fiasco, he wasn't going to risk tying Sharkey up with anything short of metal handcuffs.

Within five minutes the police that Hawk had said were on their way arrived. They handcuffed Sharkey and dragged him out of the room, while dozens of hospital staff looked on.

A third cop interrogated Hawk while Isaac righted his IV pole. Leah cuddled Ben close for several minutes before straightening up to look at Isaac.

"You're bleeding," she said. She brought a towel and pressed it over the widening patch of blood on his gown.

"Yeah, well, it was worth it." He gazed down at her blue eyes and knew in that moment he would do anything in his power to make her happy. "You and Ben should have run out of the room. There's no way he would have followed you," he chided softly.

"I couldn't bear the thought that he might have shot you or Shane in retaliation," Leah said in a husky tone. "I'm so glad you're all right, Isaac."

"I'm sorry for putting you in danger," he murmured, brushing a dark curl from her cheek. "And I wouldn't blame you if you turned and walked away from me. But I hope you don't. I want a chance to tell you how much I care about you."

"Oh, Isaac, I care about you, too. Very much."

He thought he might be dreaming, but the shimmering emotion in her eyes gave him hope. He bent his head toward her, stealing a kiss.

"Are you kissing again?" Ben asked.

Isaac regretfully lifted his head, knowing this wasn't the best time and place for this. "Yeah. Sorry. Are you okay, Ben?" When the boy nodded, he was relieved. "How about we head back to my room?" he suggested.

"Sure, but don't the police have to talk to you, too?" Leah asked, glancing over her shoulder as they left.

"They can come and find me."

Back in his room, he sat down on the edge of the bed with relief. The throbbing pain in his side had only gotten worse since he'd taken down Sharkey, but he wasn't about to complain. He'd have risked far more to put that scum away for the rest of his life.

For a few minutes there was a bevy of activity as his nurse brought his antibiotic and then called Dr. Lansing to come and look at his wound. The surgeon wasn't pleased with his handiwork being ripped open, and Leah took Ben outside the room while they quickly sutured him back together.

When mother and son returned, Hawk was with them. "I've been discharged," he announced. "And Sharkey is going to jail for a long time."

"Thank goodness," Leah murmured.

"I thought I'd take Ben down for a snack at the vending machines," Hawk continued. "How about it, buddy? You want a treat?"

"Yeah!" He jumped up and down excitedly.

Isaac suspected that Hawk was taking Ben out of there on purpose to give him and Leah some time alone. Hawk must have noticed their kiss, too, and maybe wasn't upset about him dating his sister. Isaac was grateful for his support, but the minute they left he felt tongue-tied.

"I heard your boss yelling at you earlier," Leah said, twisting the edge of her sweater with nervous fingers. "I'm sorry if I caused problems for you at work. And I hope he's not going to do anything rash."

Isaac shrugged. "Griff has always been a fair boss. I'm sure he'll do the right thing. But it doesn't matter, really, because I would do it all again if it meant keeping you and Ben safe."

"Really?" She took a tentative step toward him.

"Really." He smiled and held out his hand, relieved when she took it and came to sit beside him. "Leah, I know life has been crazy since we met again, but I care about you so much. I don't want things to end between us now that the danger is truly over."

"I don't want that, either," she confessed. "I'd like to spend more time with you."

His heart soared with a mixture of joy and relief. "I love you, Leah." The words came surprisingly easy now. "I know it might be too soon for you, but I want you to know that I'll wait for as long as it takes for you to get over losing your husband."

"You won't have to wait long," she assured him with a tremulous smile. "Because I love you, too."

"Even though I'm a cop?" he pressed.

"Yes, because I wouldn't change anything about you, Isaac. You're strong, smart, protective and great with Ben. I love you exactly the way you are."

He was almost afraid to believe her. "I promise I won't sacrifice my relationship with you and Ben for the job," he vowed. "I'll put you both first."

"Isaac, you're not the only one responsible for

the disintegration of your marriage," she said with a sad smile. "Your wife owns a piece, too. Maybe you made mistakes, but her having an affair wasn't the answer."

"I know," he agreed. "And it's taken almost dying for me to realize that you were right all along about forgiveness. If God can forgive my sins, then I have no choice but to forgive the man who took Jeremy's life. And to forgive myself. For the first time in years, I'm at peace."

"We'll be your family now," Leah said, resting her head on his shoulder. "I was so afraid to open myself up to love again, but somehow loving you makes me feel stronger instead of scared. You've taught me to be strong, Isaac."

"You were always stronger than you gave yourself credit for," he pointed out. "And you won't be sorry," he added solemnly. "I've learned from my mistakes. I'm so blessed to have you and Ben in my life."

"That goes double for me and Ben," she murmured.

Isaac turned to pull her more firmly into his arms.

And sealed their agreement with a kiss.

EPILOGUE

"Hi, Ben. How was school today?" Isaac asked as the boy raced into Leah's house.

"Supercool! One of the girls in my class got sick and threw up all over, so we didn't have to do any math!"

Isaac coughed to hide a laugh. "It's not cool that the girl was sick, Ben," he corrected.

"I know, but still, no math!"

Isaac shook his head with a wry grin and glanced at the clock. They had only a couple of hours until Leah got home from work. He'd been spending his days here, helping her with Ben, since Isaac was still on medical leave from work. Griff hadn't fired him, especially after Sharkey turned up at the hospital. And after his arrest they managed to close several open cases that were all related to the illegal gun scheme.

"Ben, listen, I want to talk to you for a minute, man-to-man," Isaac said.

"Okay." The boy followed him into the living room.

"Ben, I love your mom," Isaac began.

"Me, too," Ben said.

Isaac suppressed another chuckle. "Ah, that's good. I love your mom and I want to ask her to marry me, but I need to know if you're okay with that."

Ben scrunched up his face. "Are you going to keep kissing her?" he complained.

"Yes, I'd like to." He wasn't about to compromise that much. "But if I married your mom, I'd also be your dad." Isaac couldn't believe his future rested in the hands of an almost six-year-old.

"A real dad?" Ben asked, his eyes widening. "You'd live here with us and stay here forever and ever?"

Relief bloomed in Isaac's chest. "Yes, I'd live here with you and your mom forever and ever."

"Yay!" Ben jumped up from the sofa and rushed over to hug him.

Isaac held him tight and knew that he'd passed the first hurdle. Now he only needed to convince Leah.

"What if she says no?" Ben asked, pulling away with a frown.

"Then I'll keep asking until she says yes," Isaac assured him. "Now listen, here's the plan, okay?"

Ben giggled once he'd heard it. "Okay!"

* * *

Leah came home from work, exhausted but happy, because they'd saved a life in the trauma bay. They couldn't save them all, of course, but there was no better feeling than when they did.

"Isaac? Ben? I'm home," she announced as she stepped inside.

There were candles and three place settings of her best china on the dining room table. A bouquet of flowers sat between the candles, featuring orange blossoms, her favorite.

"What's the occasion?" she asked, making her way into the kitchen, where Isaac was stirring something tomato based on the stove. "Did you get cleared to go back to work on desk duty?"

"Next week," he confirmed. He drew her into his arms for a warm kiss. "Welcome home."

Leah blushed and pulled away from him, glancing around for Ben. "I hope you're not letting him play video games," she warned.

"No, he's cleaning his room. Ben, come and say hello to your mom," Isaac called. "Dinner will be ready in a few minutes."

She could get used to coming home to a man cooking her dinner and could admit to herself that she missed Isaac when he left every night to return home. She was grateful to have him throughout each day, but as soon as he went back to work, the pampering would end and they'd see even less of each other. "Smells delicious," she commented.

"Ben said your favorite meal was spaghetti."

She laughed. "Yes, and it just so happens to be Ben's favorite, too."

"Sit down at the table. I'll bring everything in," Isaac said.

"All right." She brushed another kiss across his lips and then headed into the dining room. She sat down and smiled as Ben came into the room.

"Hi, Mom." He greeted her with a hug.

"Hi, yourself," she teased, kissing the top of his head before letting him wiggle free.

"We have a surprise for you," Ben announced as Isaac brought in a bowl of pasta.

"Wait a minute, Ben," Isaac warned. "I don't have everything ready yet."

"Hurry up," he said impatiently, hopping from one foot to the other.

Leah frowned, wondering what was going on. The two men in her life had cooked up some sort of surprise, but what? It wasn't her birthday, or Ben's, although his was less than a month away. But was it Isaac's? She was horrified that she didn't know and made a mental note to ask.

"Here's the spaghetti sauce and the garlic bread," Isaac announced as he set the items on the table. "Now, Ben."

Her son came over to her left side, while Isaac

knelt beside her chair on the right. When she saw the small velvet ring box in Isaac's hand, her heart tripped and stumbled in her chest.

"Mom, will you marry Isaac? Please?"

Isaac audibly sighed. "Ben, you were supposed to let me ask her first," he pointed out gently.

"Oops. Sorry."

"Leah, will you please marry me?"

"Yes, Isaac, I'd love to marry you." She blinked away tears as he slid the diamond ring onto her finger.

"Yay, now I have a real dad!" Ben exclaimed.

Leah smiled and allowed Isaac to draw her to her feet and pull her close.

"And I'll have an amazing family," Isaac murmured before he lowered his head and claimed her mouth with his.

She kissed him back, thankful that God had given them both a second chance at love.

* * * * *

Dear Reader,

Welcome to my new miniseries SWAT: Top Cops! Over the years we've heard so many terrible tragedies related to mass shootings, and I wanted to honor the brave men and women who risk their lives to keep the rest of us safe. Meeting some of our local SWAT team members in person gave me the idea to write a miniseries about them.

Under the Lawman's Protection is the third book in the series. Isaac Morrison has a special talent for being a hostage negotiator, but still lives with the guilt of not being able to save his young son. When a friend asks for help in protecting his sister, Leah Nichols, and her five-year-old son, Ben, Isaac arrives just in time to prevent them from being kidnapped at gunpoint. After a second attempt on Leah's life a few hours later, Isaac is determined to do whatever possible to keep her and Ben safe. Leah has guarded her heart for years, since her husband died. Can Isaac and Leah put their painful losses aside to rejoice in finding love a second time around?

I hope you enjoyed reading Isaac and Leah's story. I'm always thrilled and honored to hear from my readers, and I can be reached through my website at www.laurascottbooks.com, on

Facebook at Laura Scott Books and on Twitter, @laurascottbooks.

Yours in faith,
Laura Scott

Questions for Discussion

1. In the beginning of the story, Leah is determined to keep her distance from Isaac because he's a cop and her father died in the line of duty. Do you think her fear is irrational? Why or why not?

2. Isaac comes from a troubled past and doesn't think he's good enough for a woman like Leah. Describe how faith could help Isaac deal with his past in a better way.

3. Leah wants Isaac to help her brother, Shane, but Isaac believes that his first priority should be to keep Leah and Ben safe. Discuss a time when you were torn between two emotional choices.

4. Isaac begins to pray when he's faced with a dangerous, life-threatening situation. Discuss a troubled time in your life when you might have turned to prayer for support.

5. Isaac soon believes that a dirty cop might be responsible for the danger threatening Leah and Ben. Discuss a time when someone close to you betrayed your trust.

6. Isaac learns to have faith in God and accepts that his dead son is in a much better place. Describe a time when you lost someone close to you and how you helped deal with that loss.

LARGER-PRINT BOOKS!

GET 2 FREE
LARGER-PRINT NOVELS
PLUS 2 FREE
MYSTERY GIFTS

Love Inspired®

SUSPENSE
RIVETING INSPIRATIONAL ROMANCE

Larger-print novels are now available...